"Have you thought about my proposal?"

She'd like to tell him no, to pretend her every thought hadn't revolved around him for the last twenty-four hours. Unfortunately, she'd never been that good an actress. "I'm still thinking."

A sensual smile tilted up one corner of his mouth. "Perhaps you need more persuading." His husky tone suggested what form his influence would take.

The heat spiraling through her body tempted her to vacillate just so she could feel his mouth against her for real. Last night's dream had left her unfulfilled. Given half a chance, Alex would take care of that problem.

At a price.

She understood the unspoken terms. Marriage or nothing.

Dear Reader,

April showers are bringing flowers—and a soul-stirring bouquet of dream-come-true stories from Silhouette Romance!

Red Rose needs men! And it's up to Ellie Donahue to put the town-ladies' plans into action—even if it means enticing her secret love to return to his former home. Inspired by classic legends, Myrna Mackenzie's new miniseries, THE BRIDES OF RED ROSE, begins with Ellie's tale, in *The Pied Piper's Bride* (SR #1714).

Bestselling author Judy Christenberry brings you another Wild West story in her FROM THE CIRCLE K miniseries. In *The Last Crawford Bachelor* (SR #1715), lawyer Michael Crawford—the family's last single son—meets his match...and is then forced to live with her on the Circle K!

And this lively bunch of spring stories wouldn't be complete without Teresa Carpenter's *Daddy's Little Memento* (SR #1716). School nurse Samantha Dell reunites her infant nephew with his handsome father, only to learn that if she wants to retain custody then she's got to say, "I do"! And then there's Colleen Faulkner's *Barefoot and Pregnant?* (SR #1717), in which career-woman Elise Montgomery has everything a girl could want—except the man of her dreams. Will she find a husband where she least expects him?

All the best,

Mavis C. Allen
Associate Senior Editor

Please address questions and book requests to:
Silhouette Reader Service
U.S.: 3010 Walden Ave., P.O. Box 1325, Buffalo, NY 14269
Canadian: P.O. Box 609, Fort Erie, Ont. L2A 5X3

Daddy's Little Memento

TERESA CARPENTER

SILHOUETTE *Romance*®

Published by Silhouette Books

America's Publisher of Contemporary Romance

In loving memory of Charles Joseph Carpenter.
Daddy, you'll always be my hero.

 SILHOUETTE BOOKS

ISBN 0-373-19716-0

DADDY'S LITTLE MEMENTO

Copyright © 2004 by Teresa Carpenter

All rights reserved. Except for use in any review, the reproduction or utilization of this work in whole or in part in any form by any electronic, mechanical or other means, now known or hereafter invented, including xerography, photocopying and recording, or in any information storage or retrieval system, is forbidden without the written permission of the editorial office, Silhouette Books, 233 Broadway, New York, NY 10279 U.S.A.

All characters in this book have no existence outside the imagination of the author and have no relation whatsoever to anyone bearing the same name or names. They are not even distantly inspired by any individual known or unknown to the author, and all incidents are pure invention.

This edition published by arrangement with Harlequin Books S.A.

® and TM are trademarks of Harlequin Books S.A., used under license. Trademarks indicated with ® are registered in the United States Patent and Trademark Office, the Canadian Trade Marks Office and in other countries.

Visit Silhouette at www.eHarlequin.com

Printed in U.S.A.

Books by Teresa Carpenter

Silhouette Special Edition

The Baby Due Date #1260

Silhouette Romance

Daddy's Little Memento #1716

TERESA CARPENTER

is a fifth-generation Californian who currently lives amid the chaos of her family in San Diego. She loves living there because she can travel for thirty minutes and be either in the mountains or at the beach. She began her love affair with romances in the seventh grade when she talked her mother into buying her a category romance; she and romance have been together ever since.

Teresa has worked in the banking and mortgage industry for fifteen years. When not working or writing, she likes to spend time with her nieces and nephew, go to the movies and read. A member of RWA/San Diego, she has participated on the chapter board in numerous positions, including president, VP Programs, newsletter editor and conference coordinator. She is especially proud of having received the chapter's prestigious Barbara Faith Award.

Dear Samantha,

If you're reading this letter, it means I'm gone and it's only you and Gabe now. I hope you'll find comfort in each other, as you both gave me comfort when I needed it most.

How I've envied you your strength and sense of purpose. I was weak, always so weak. And yes, I made mistakes.

You were right. I should have told Gabe's father about him. But he couldn't miss someone he never knew, and I needed Gabe so much. He's the only thing I ever did right in my life. He's my heart and my soul. I couldn't give him up.

But no more stalling, Gabe's father is Alexander Sullivan of Paradise Pines, California. I have no proof to offer you beyond a mother's knowledge. He made a point of being careful; we both did. But Gabe was meant to be. I'll always be grateful for the time I had with my son.

I rest easy knowing you'll always be there for Gabe.

Love,

Sarah

Chapter One

Alex Sullivan was a man who didn't appreciate surprises.

He believed in rules. Being the oldest of six boys, he'd learned early in life that rules created control from chaos. Being the principal of Paradise Pines High School, he knew control meant the difference between order and anarchy.

So when he opened his door on Sunday morning to find Samantha Dell, the new school nurse, standing on the front deck of his mountain home with a baby in her arms he saw trouble in tight jeans.

"Good morning, Alex." She graced him with an overbright smile.

"Hello, Samantha," he greeted the leggy blonde, fighting to control the quick surge of wanting that hit every time he looked into her lively green eyes.

He had a strict personal policy against dating colleagues, a policy she challenged twice a week. Technically, she didn't work for him, but as the district nurse, she spent two days a week at his high school, which in his mind put her off-limits.

And if that wasn't enough to put a damper on his desire, the chubby-cheeked kid she held would be.

With some regret he pulled his customary defenses in place and lifted his glance from the sweet curve of her hips up over a pale pink sweater cropped at the waist to her anxious jade-green gaze. Then, almost objectively, he studied the dark-haired, blue-eyed baby in her arms, wondering what brought the pair to his home on a cold January morning.

"Alex, I need to talk to you." Nerves wore at the edges of Samantha's smile. She cleared her throat. "May I come in?"

"Sure."

He glanced down at his T-shirt and shorts still damp from his morning run. Hardly ideal for entertaining. Sundays were his day of excess. He slept an extra hour, ran an extra mile and drank an extra cup of coffee or two while reading the paper. Sunday nights meant dinner at Gram's. Between the paper and dinner he occupied himself with everything and nothing, whatever struck his fancy.

If he was occasionally lonely, most of the time he appreciated the peace and quiet of his life.

Samantha's expression warned him his peace was about to be destroyed.

"Come on in." He stepped aside. He'd seen her with the boy, who couldn't be more than a year old, around town, but Alex always managed to keep his distance. "Is this your son?"

In the entry she turned to face him, her arms tightening around the little boy until he wiggled in her grasp.

"No. He's yours," she said in a rush.

Disbelief rooted him in place. She couldn't mean that the way it sounded. At a loss, he looked from her to the baby then back at her. "Mine, how?"

She blinked as if surprised by his question, but she quickly recovered. "Yours, as in you fathered him."

"That's not possible." Denial came first, sharp and sure. He always, always protected himself. "I only met you four months ago."

"I'm not his mother, but you are his father." Her voice was quietly earnest, compassion lit her direct gaze. "I know this must come as a surprise."

"Try shock."

She was serious. This wasn't some kind of joke. Sudden panic sent adrenaline coursing through his blood. His head went up, his shoulders went back and he stood braced to fight. He felt as if his whole life was being threatened.

Samantha reacted to his aggressive stance by taking a large step back and eyeing him with caution.

Seeing he'd frightened her, he fought for control. Determined to rule his emotions, he wiped the frown from his face and waved her into the living room.

After a brief hesitation, she led the way into the next room then perched on the edge of his black-leather couch and settled the baby on her lap. She swept an affectionate hand over downy-soft brown hair. The baby turned to grin at her then stuffed two fingers in his mouth.

Alex chose the matching chair several feet away. In the four months he'd known her, he'd found her to be intelligent, dedicated and friendly with most people, if a little distant with him. He figured her reserve came from the same belief he held that you shouldn't mix business with pleasure.

Eyeing the little guy in the red T-shirt, miniature overalls and baby Reeboks, he didn't know what to think.

All he saw when he looked into those baby-blue eyes was years of responsibility. As the oldest, Alex had done his baby duty and helped with his five younger brothers when he'd still been a child himself. He'd been fourteen when his parents died in an earthquake in South America, making him the man of the family. They were supposed to have been on a buying trip for the family jewelry store but they'd been on an archeological excavation instead. They'd paid the price for playing when they should have been working. But Alex and his brothers were the ones who suffered.

To this day sorrow at their loss mixed with feelings of resentment.

Thank God for Gram, she took them in, provided a home and worked overtime to hold the business together. Alex did his best to hold the *family* together.

Make no mistake, he loved his brothers. He also loved kids, as principal of the high school he had to, but the thought of going home to one after spending eight hours with four-hundred teenagers blew his mind.

Not that he believed for a millisecond the boy was his.

"Who's the kid, Samantha?" he demanded. Again. Hoping for a different explanation, one that made sense.

"Gabe is eleven months old." She licked her bottom lip, the gesture revealing an underlying uncertainty. One she tried to hide by lifting her chin and meeting his gaze straight on. "He's my nephew." She tensed as if bracing herself. "And he *is* your son."

He pushed to his feet. He wished she'd stop saying that.

"I don't have any children. By choice." And by God's will.

With a pang, he pushed the thought away.

He saw he'd startled her, but she quickly recovered. "You may not have meant to, but you did. According to my sister's letter, you met at a Caribbean resort the summer before last."

She named the resort on St. Thomas where he'd vacationed nearly two years ago. A quiver of dread ran down his spine. So she had the time and place right, but that didn't mean the boy was his.

"What's your sister's name? Why didn't she tell me herself?"

"Her name was Sarah Travis. We were half sisters. She died in an automobile accident six months ago."

Sarah. He had the impression of flashing green eyes, short sassy curls and a wanton wildness in bed. She'd been just what he needed to take his mind off one of the darkest moments in his life.

"I remember your sister. I'm sorry to hear of her death. But you're mistaken about Gabe. He's not my son."

"Duck." Gabe pointed a chubby finger toward a marble statue of birds in flight. "Duck. Duck."

"Pretty birdies." Samantha pulled the baby's hand to her mouth and pretended to bite his finger, then kissed the mock injury. Gabe laughed and stuck his finger in her mouth. She repeated the game then turned her attention back to Alex. Her love for the little boy showed in her tender handling of him even as she pursued the serious conversation.

"My sister was a bit of a free spirit, but she didn't lie. In fact, she refused to reveal who you were while she was alive. It wasn't until after she passed away that I found a letter in her safe-deposit box naming you as Gabe's father."

"No disrespect to the dead, but your sister was wrong." He paced, his agitation requiring a release. "We only spent two nights together, and I used protection. I always use protection."

Samantha lifted a darkened brow. "You're the principal of a high school, you know as well as I do the only one-hundred-percent effective birth control is abstinence. Condoms can break or fail." The spark in her green eyes warned Alex she wouldn't listen to any criticism of her sister. She cleared her throat then continued. "You are Gabe's father."

Alex rubbed at the ache building in his left temple. He wasn't convinced, but she obviously believed what she told him. Which brought him to his next burning question.

"You've been in Paradise Pines for four months. Why are you just telling me now? Come to that, why didn't your sister tell me when she found out she was pregnant?"

Pink bloomed in her cheeks, and she busied herself with Gabe's clothes, straightening the overall straps over the red shirt and refolding the cuffs of his socks. Gabe put up with the fussing for about twenty seconds before bucking his small body, demanding to be put down. In his struggle, his hand caught in the neck of her sweater dragging it down.

Alex's breath hitched at the sight of cream lace cupping creamier flesh. Samantha quickly righted the garment, flashing him a self-conscious look. No need. He'd already noticed her trim little figure, and she had nothing to be embarrassed about.

She tried to calm Gabe, but he bucked harder and squealed, fighting her efforts.

For a moment, Alex's gaze connected with the child's blue eyes. Sullivan blue? His will and determination certainly matched that of any Sullivan.

"Let him down," Alex urged.

Samantha sent a doubtful look around the room at the glass-and-chrome tables, a high-tech entertainment center and the book-lined floor-to-ceiling shelves. "I don't think that's a good idea."

"Can he walk?"

"Not yet, but he's getting braver every day."

"Let him down. I'm sure we can catch him before he does damage to himself or anything in the room." He resumed his seat, leaving the space open for the kid.

Setting Gabe on his butt in the middle of the floor, she pulled a whiffle ball from her purse for him to play with. She gathered the scattered magazines and videos on the coffee table into a stack in the middle then resumed her seat on the edge of the couch. After a moment, she slid Alex a sidelong look before finally answering his question.

"You have to understand ours isn't the most impressive family tree," she said with a total lack of emotion that spoke volumes. "My father died when I was four, my mother when I was nineteen. Sarah's father left. Seven months before she was born. My mother wasn't a woman who found it easy to be alone. Men came into our lives, but they didn't stay.

"Sarah was twelve years old when mom died, leaving her in my care. I did the best I could, but between college and work I couldn't give Sarah all the attention she needed. By the time she met you, Sarah desperately needed to be needed. And she'd decided a baby would fulfill that need."

Alex didn't know how to respond to her revealing confession, because regardless of the sad circumstances of her life—Sarah's life—he hadn't heard an acceptable reason for not telling him he'd fathered a child.

Her expression apologetic, Samantha explained. "I'm sorry, but Sarah never intended to tell you. She went to the island with the intention of getting pregnant." She stopped, cleared her throat. Then she set her chin as if coming to a decision. "In the letter she left she said you told her you didn't want children, so she felt no need to tell you."

Shock froze Alex in place. Fury pumped blood through his veins so fast rational thought became impossible. Not again. Damn it, no, not again.

He felt as if an essential part of him had been ripped out, stolen, used.

When he didn't speak, Samantha answered the second part of his question. "Perhaps I should have told you sooner. But it took a while to get settled and for Gabe and me to develop a routine. And I needed to get to know you."

Already angry, he resented the implied insult. He narrowed his eyes and pinned her with a cold glare. "Are you saying I had to pass some kind of test?"

She shrugged but made no apology. "From the moment I found out she was pregnant I urged Sarah to notify the baby's father. She resisted until the end. When Gabe suddenly came into my care and the decision became mine, I felt I had to honor my first instinct to contact you."

"But?"

"But," her tone became defensive, "now he's my responsibility and his welfare is my first concern."

"Meaning?" Alex consciously relaxed his clenched jaw. How crazy was it to be angry that she hadn't told him sooner about the child he denied was his?

"Meaning, I believe no father is better than an abusive father."

He leaned forward in his chair. "It happens I agree with you. What bothers me is it took you four months to decide I don't hurt little kids."

"Of course it didn't take four months—Gabe, no."

The baby had crawled to the coffee table, hoisted himself up and was happily slapping the glass. "He's getting antsy. I'd better go."

Alex watched in disbelief as she rose, picked up Gabe and headed for the door.

"Wait." He followed hot on her heels. "Why did you come here today? What do you want?"

She stopped in the open door, her expression no longer anxious but relieved. "I came to tell you about your son. I hope you'll want to be part of his life. What happens next is up to you." When he had no answer to that, she turned away. "Goodbye."

He continued to watch her walk away, stunned into speechlessness.

The boy had the last word. He looked at Alex over his aunt's shoulder with solemn blue eyes much like Alex's own and said, "Bye-bye."

"Well that didn't go as badly as I'd feared." Samantha snuggled Gabe against her chest and kissed his dark curls as she descended the deck steps. "Disbelief and shock were expected. But he didn't deny knowing your mom and he didn't throw us out. That's good."

"Mama." Gabe grinned and patted her cheek.

Mama. Her heart twisted every time he used the word. She felt like a fake, as if she were stealing her sister's place in the world. Every day she did her best to keep Sarah alive for Gabe. But because it was easiest for him, Samantha answered to mama.

"I probably should have told him about you sooner, but we needed the time together, didn't we, sweetheart.'' Digging into her purse, she pulled out her keys and hit the unlock button on her alarm pad.

''In you go.'' She opened the back door of her Taurus and fit Gabe into his car seat. After snapping him in and handing him his toy giraffe, she crouched in the open door.

''We'll give your father some time and see what happens. He's a decent guy. I know he cares about his family and his students, so how can he resist you?'' Gabe giggled when she bussed his nose. ''We did what we came to do. The rest is up to him. Raising your mother alone was the hardest thing I've ever done. And I'm not too proud to say I need help.''

''Man?'' Gabe yawned.

''Right.'' She smiled and chucked him under the chin. ''Your dad's the man all right. I hope he comes through because, from what I remember, having a daddy was one of the best things in the world.''

Samantha's biggest regret was not remembering her father better. Mustache kisses, unconditional love and being safe, that's what she remembered. No wonder her mom had missed him so much.

''Samantha.''

Startled she stood and spun to find Alex standing on the deck above her. He appeared larger than life with his broad shoulders silhouetted against the gray morning sky. His features were shadowed, hiding his expression, but his dark hair showed signs of his frustration, actually standing on end.

She felt herself pale as she worried, had he heard her talking to Gabe?

Thrusting his hands in his pockets, Alex said, ''I

want a DNA test. I'll pick you and Gabe up tomorrow at four.''

She disliked his autocratic tone, but she didn't protest. His asking for the test showed his willingness to believe. Okay, it could also be considered an opportunity to disprove her claim, but she preferred to be positive.

Truthfully, it was more than she'd hoped for so soon. So let him be demanding. Gabe and she had nothing to lose and everything to gain.

''We'll be ready.''

Samantha eyed Alex who brooded in the corner of the exam room. He stood, arms crossed, shoulder propped against the wall, trying to appear relaxed and failing. His pale complexion and tapping foot betrayed his unease.

Like father, like son. Gabe's inability to sit still in her lap showed his tension as they all waited for the doctor.

''Are you okay?'' she asked Alex, knowing many people had an aversion to visiting the doctor.

He arched an eyebrow with forced nonchalance. ''I'm fine.''

''We don't have to do this you know. You could take my word Gabe is your son.''

He actually hesitated before shaking his head. ''I think it's best we know for certain.''

''Mama.'' Gabe fussed. He twisted in her arms turning to face her, but when she gathered him close, he pushed against her in a bid to get down.

''No, Gabe, you have to stay with me. It shouldn't

be long before the doctor is here.'' The apprehension in the room getting to her, she glanced at Alex standing in his corner. ''Will it?''

''He'll be here soon.''

So he'd said twenty minutes ago. If Alex had allowed the nurse to gather the DNA sample, they'd have been done and gone by now. Heck, she could have done the job herself with him as a witness. But no, he had to have his doctor friend do the deed. He didn't trust anyone else.

Fine. With Gabe's future at stake she accepted the need for precautions and exactness.

Still, Samantha gritted her teeth, seeking patience. Even understanding the need to know, it was hard to stay calm when Gabe's wiggling and whining made every minute seem like ten.

''Look at the boat, Gabe.'' Hoping to distract the baby, she pointed to the large framed photograph of a sailboat on the wall. ''See the boat.''

Gabe stilled. He looked from her face to the picture. ''Bo.''

''Yes. Boat.'' Thrilled at his new word, she kissed him. ''Good boy. Soon we'll go to the beach like I promised, and I'll show you the real boats on the water.''

''I have a boat.'' The low words came from Alex's corner.

Samantha sent him a surprised look. Was he just making conversation to distract himself, or was he issuing an invitation?

Seeing the blank look he aimed at the test kit, she had her answer. Neither she nor Gabe would be zipping across the waves anytime soon. Which in no way detracted from Gabe's triumph.

"Boat is a new word for him," she boasted.

"Bo? That was boat?"

She grinned. "Sometimes you have to use a little imagination."

"Ah."

The door opened and the doctor walked in. Tall, with white-blond hair cut short and wide shoulders, he reminded Samantha of Mr. Clean in a lab coat. Alex introduced his friend as Dr. Douglas Wilcox. The doctor apologized for keeping them waiting, and Alex thanked him for helping them out on such short notice.

Pleasantries aside, Dr. Wilcox went right to work. Samantha held Gabe, who cried and refused to open his mouth for the swab. Luckily the doctor knew his business and was quick. He praised Gabe and covered a freckle on his arm with a Superman Band-Aid.

While the baby inspected his badge of courage Dr. Wilcox labeled the samples. Then he gestured for Alex to take a seat.

"I guess I don't have to ask if you're nervous. My cadaver has more color than you."

"Ha ha. I thought this was done with a blood test." Alex sent his friend a killer look. Doug knew how he hated visits to the doctor. Alex figured the hang-up came from having to drag his brothers to their appointments when he didn't like going any better than they did. The possible outcome of the test results didn't help settle his nerves, either.

"Didn't I tell you? DNA tests are done with swabs

these days. No needles today.'' Doug winked at Samantha, a totally uncalled-for gesture in Alex's opinion.

He frowned. "Let's just get this over with."

Doug demanded Alex say ah. Conscious of her eyes on him, he complied. Doug swabbed the inside of Alex's cheek twice. Doug then labeled two plastic vials and placed one of the swabs in each of the envelopes already holding Gabe's samples.

Two envelopes, one Doug would send to a lab, the other for Samantha to have tested through her own sources. There would be no doubt of the results.

Finally. The ordeal was almost over.

He thanked the Lord, only to have Samantha drop twenty pounds of baby in his lap.

"Watch Gabe for a minute, will you? I have to use the rest room." Samantha zipped out the door.

"Wait," Alex protested uselessly. He held Gabe by the waist with his feet dangling below him. "She couldn't hold it for a minute?"

Doug grinned from where he stood completing his instructions for the lab. "If you've got to go, you've got to go."

Alex glared at his friend. "You're just a laugh a minute today."

"I call 'em as I see 'em." Doug pulled up a stool and sat down across from Alex. "Cute kid. Looks a lot like you. He has your eyes and your chin."

Alex turned Gabe this way and that, studying him. The baby liked this new game, kicking his feet and laughing. He reached out and grabbed Alex by the hair, shrieking with glee. "Man."

"I don't see the resemblance." Alex carefully worked his hair free. Gabe giggled and kicked harder. "So he has blue eyes. All babies have blue eyes."

"Not by this age." The doctor denied Alex's statement.

"Well it's common, as is brown hair, lots of men have that coloring," Alex said, suppressing a smile at Gabe's antics.

"He has his mother's nose."

Alex arched a brow. "Samantha's his aunt, not his mother."

"I know, you told me," Doug said. "He still has her nose, which means he got it from his mother. Genetics work that way."

"You're not helping." Alex advised his grinning friend. He had to admit, though, that Gabe's button nose reminded him of Samantha's.

"Samantha's a beautiful woman," Doug commented with a little more interest in his tone than Alex cared for.

He sent the other man a warning glare. "Forget it."

All innocence, Doug crossed his arms over his chest. "Why, because you saw her first?"

"Yes." Not that Alex intended doing anything about his attraction, but the situation was way too complicated to add anyone else to the equation.

He lowered Gabe until the little boy's feet rested on Alex's thighs. Now instead of kicking, the baby bounced. "He's a strong little guy."

"He appears happy. And healthy," the doctor observed, reaching out to pat the kid on the head.

Gabe turned to see who was patting his head and

seeing Doug, his face scrunched up and he shied back against Alex.

"No," Gabe said loud and clear. "Bad man."

Alex laughed along with Doug.

"He doesn't like you." Alex ran a soothing hand over Gabe's back. "I don't blame you, kid. He's the man who pokes and prods, huh?"

Alex could definitely relate. But when Gabe laid his head on Alex's shoulder, he felt a sinking feeling in his gut. Better his gut than his heart. He didn't want to have anything in common with the baby. Not blue eyes, brown hair or a fear of doctors.

The point of this visit, these tests, was to disprove Alex's paternity. Then he'd have no more to do with Gabe. Or his pretty aunt Samantha.

Life would return to the peace and orderliness Alex craved, and he'd put this disturbing event behind him.

And hope for no more surprises.

Peace. That's what he wanted. Wasn't it?

Chapter Two

Samantha's rubber soles made soft swishing sounds against the tile floor of the deserted high-school corridor. Alex had sent a note asking to see her after school let out.

Not, she suspected, as principal to school nurse but as Gabe's father to Gabe's aunt.

Butterflies beat a wild tattoo in her stomach, a sign of her heightened anxiety. In the two weeks since she told Alex about Gabe, they hadn't been on the friendliest of terms. Waiting for the test results made them both tense.

Perhaps she should have told him about Gabe sooner.

In her defense, parenting didn't come easily. Whoever said it did, lied. It certainly hadn't the first time when she'd gained custody of Sarah. So far, this time was no different. Except she was older, thirty-one instead of nineteen.

And this time she hoped not to do it alone.

Pressing a hand against her stomach to tamp down the havoc caused by anticipation and nervousness, she tapped on Alex's door.

"Come in," he called in his deep velvet voice, the voice that made her hormones sit up and take notice.

She stepped inside and closed the door, bracing herself, because every time their eyes met a zing of awareness curled all the way down to her toes.

He sat behind a large desk, his dark head bent over a stack of papers. George Washington stared down from the wall. The American flag stood in the corner. Alex's sleeves were rolled up and his tie loosened. The breadth of his shoulders filled the executive chair he sat in and his hair-dusted forearms bracketed the document he studied.

Even disheveled he took her breath.

Which made his inattention aggravating. He had asked for this meeting, the least he could do was attend it.

"Alex," she prompted as she took a seat in one of the hardwood chairs facing him. "You wanted to see me?"

"Yes. I'm sorry, I just want to finish this." He signed his name at the bottom of the paper then set it aside and looked up.

And zing, her toes curled in her white, rubber-soled shoes. She knew he felt the attraction, too. Desire blazed in his blue, blue eyes. A flash of hunger quickly banked.

Unfortunately, knowing changed nothing. Because acting on the attraction would be downright insane.

Darn it.

Scowling, he blinked away all signs of passion, then ran a hand over the back of his neck. The weariness in his gesture distracted Samantha. He usually seemed so vital, so in control.

Seeing him at less than his normal hundred-and-ten percent made her want to tend to him. Fighting the urge, she linked her fingers together. Best she keep her hands and nurturing instincts to herself.

Without meaning to, she heard herself ask, "Tough day?"

He shrugged, a frown drawing his eyebrows together. "No worse than usual." He tossed his pen on the desk and leaned back in his chair. "Speculation about Gabe is starting to get around. I got a call from a member of the school board."

"Oh." Guilt assailed Samantha. What could she say? "Do you feel Gabe's illegitimacy will reflect badly on you?"

She really hoped Alex would say no. But even with San Diego only thirty miles down the highway, Paradise Pines was a small town, with small-town values and small-town ethics. As principal, and the highest adult influence on their children, the citizens could be disturbed to learn Alex had an illegitimate child.

For the first time since she entered his office, he smiled. "Paradise Pines isn't that provincial." His expression turned rueful. "At least I don't think it is." He stood and came around the desk. "We'll know soon enough. That's why I called you in here, to tell you I received the results of the DNA tests."

She caught her breath. "Really? My lab said four

to six weeks for the results.'' Mixed feelings made her heart pound. She believed her sister believed Alex was the father of her child. Heck, Samantha had based major decisions on that belief, but the test results were official. ''So?''

''Gabe is my son.''

Her breath escaped in a rush of relief. Finally. Now they could move forward. Samantha tried to gauge Alex's reaction, but his matter-of-fact manner gave her no clue to his true feelings.

Keeping his serious gaze on hers, he clasped his hands in front of him and leaned back against his desk. ''You need to know, Samantha, that I've hired an attorney. I'm petitioning for custody.''

Shock rocked Samantha. She stared, trying to wrap her mind around what she'd heard. Alex couldn't have said he meant to take Gabe away from her.

''No,'' she protested, denying her worst fears. ''You can't have him.'' Needing to hold on to something solid, she clutched the wooden arms of her chair. ''Gabe belongs with me.''

''You're upset.'' He reached for her hand, but she pulled away from him.

She laughed harshly. ''Of course I'm upset. Did you expect me to be happy to have you steal him from me?''

He arched a dark eyebrow in a silent reminder that his claim to Gabe was stronger than hers. ''I expect you to want what's best for him.''

''I do.'' She congratulated herself on the restraint that kept her from slapping the arrogant look from his face. "I don't believe taking him from the only family he's ever known constitutes what's best."

"I'm not taking him from you," he denied in exasperation.

"No?" she mocked him. "You're seeking custody. What would you call it?"

He shifted his position against the desk, crossed his ankles and leaned back. "Gabe is my son, my responsibility."

"I commend you on your sense of duty." With her heart being torn in two, she couldn't prevent the sarcasm. She crossed her arms over her breasts, more to contain the fresh wave of pain than out of defiance. "But you need more than duty to raise a baby. You need love and patience and understanding."

He glanced around his office then back at her. "I'm aware of what it takes to raise a child."

"There's more to raising a child than education." Feeling cornered, she stood and hugged herself as she paced. "Why didn't you tell me about this sooner?"

"I didn't have the test results. My attorney only filed the petition today."

"But you knew what you were planning," she accused, remembering with a sense of betrayal how pleased she'd been at his willingness to have the DNA tests done. Little had she known he'd use the results to undermine her position as Gabe's guardian.

Her heart rose to her throat as she realized she had no legal claim to Gabe. His care had passed from her sister to Samantha by right of family taking care of family. Nobody had questioned her custody. Until now, when it might be too late to protect Gabe's interests.

"You're right." Alex looked her straight in the eye, challenging her. "I should have told you of my intentions sooner. Just as you should have told me Gabe was my son earlier."

Oh no, he wasn't going to make her feel guilty.

She'd turned her life upside down to bring his son to him. Maybe Alex was right. Maybe the decision to wait hadn't been fair. But she'd needed to know in her heart that introducing Gabe to Alex was not only right, but safe.

This wasn't supposed to happen. She'd never dreamed he'd try to take Gabe from her. In her experience, men didn't stay around to raise their own children. And she'd learned the hard way—when her fiancé left her rather than help with Sarah—that they didn't care to take on the raising of other men's kids, either.

Heaven knew she'd hoped Alex would take an interest in Gabe, but deep down she hadn't really believed he would.

"You didn't believe me when I did tell you." She voiced her outrage. "You have no right to blame me for trying to protect Gabe. I gave up a job I'd had for five years and moved him to a new state so he could meet his father. Don't tell me I haven't done my part. It takes time to—"

Alex held up a hand. "All right. Calm down."

"Do not patronize me." Seething with temper, her breasts heaving with the force of restraining her anger, Samantha informed him, "I won't let you take him from me."

"It's done. The papers have been filed."

She clenched her teeth, bracing herself against the anxiety his words instilled. "I'll fight you. My sister made it clear she wanted him raised by her family."

His eyebrows lowered. "Your sister's wishes don't concern me. She had no right to use me for stud services then hide my son from me. I believe the courts will agree."

"So that's why you're doing this," she responded to his bitter claim. "To get back at my sister? And I suppose it doesn't matter that Gabe will be hurt by your actions?"

"Gabe is my main concern. He needs a stable home."

"He has a stable home." Agitated, she paced to the bookcase then back. "He's a good baby, but taking him from the family he's become accustomed to will only upset and confuse him. Even traumatize him."

"I'm his father. I am family," he said, not unkindly. "He's young, with the right structure and guidance he'll adjust."

Samantha cringed, his words like a dagger to her heart. "I love him," she challenged Alex. "Can you say the same?"

Silent, he stared at her.

The shrill ring of the phone broke the tense moment. He frowned at the interruption. She watched his internal struggle, but in the end duty won. He rounded the desk and snatched up the receiver. "Sullivan."

She headed for the door. Wanting to escape, to rethink and regroup. And to plan what to do next. Let him take his call. She was out of there.

"Samantha."

The authority in his voice stopped her. Reluctantly, she half-turned, looking at him over her shoulder.

He stood with his hand over the mouthpiece, his expression resolute. "I haven't been given the opportunity to love him. Isn't that why you brought him to me?"

Stricken, she turned away. That's exactly why she'd brought Gabe to him.

In the hall, she slumped against the wall, her heart in shreds as she thought of the hard man on the other side of the door. He threatened all the family she had left.

Gabe had someone fighting for him. But she feared she'd be the one to lose.

On Saturday Samantha secured the strap on Gabe's car seat, dodging his busy fists to do so. She'd told him about Alex's bid for custody, but of course he didn't understand. He didn't worry, as she did, that their time together might be limited. "I should just pack you up and run away with you. Then he couldn't take you from me."

"Ducky. Ducky," Gabe said hopefully.

"That's right." Smiling at his one-track mind, Samantha chucked him under the chin. "We're going to feed the duckies."

He'd been cranky with teething pains today, and since the sunny afternoon had chased away the morning chill, she'd promised him a trip to the pond to distract him.

Thank goodness he didn't understand. He deserved happiness and security. As long as he was with her, that's what he'd get.

After handing him a cookie and making sure the bag of bread crumbs was out of his reach, she straightened from the back seat and closed the door. Turning, she practically stubbed her nose on Alex's chest.

"Oh!" she exclaimed in surprise. Reacting to his nearness, she took a quick step back from the breadth of him, from the soap and male smell of him. And promptly found her fanny pressed up against the car.

Dread landed heavy in her stomach. Had he heard her thoughtless comment about running away?

"What are you doing here?" she asked with more bite than she'd intended.

"I came to see Gabe." Alex tucked his hands in his pants pockets, taupe Dockers topped by a navy polo shirt, and stood his ground. His stance effectively blocked her path. "It looks like you have plans."

Was he baiting her? Unwilling to play mouse to his cat, she addressed the issue directly. "I'm not going to run with him."

He lifted a dark eyebrow, but he didn't really look surprised. "I didn't think you would."

"But you heard me?"

"Yes," he said, looking beyond her to where Gabe began to fidget in his car seat.

"You don't sound too concerned," she responded, wondering whether to be pleased or insulted by his lack of reaction. Did he trust her or consider her so minor a threat he needn't worry?

He shrugged. "Unlike your sister, you have too much integrity to run."

Did she? Or did she simply lack the courage? Apparently he had more faith in her than she had in herself. "You sound pretty sure of that."

From less than a foot away, he looked her straight in the eyes. "You would never have brought him to my attention if you didn't believe he needed me."

She had no answer against the truth, a truth that had driven her to move more than four-hundred miles and landed her in this bind. Refusing to admit he'd touched a nerve, she moved sideways and opened the driver's door, sliding behind the wheel.

"We're going to Paradise Pond to feed the ducks. You can come if you want."

"Fee' ducky!" Gabe demanded from the back.

Alex rounded the front of the car and slid in next to her.

They traveled the few miles to their destination in silence. The walking trail surrounding Paradise Pond had been revamped when the sports center and a picnic area were built up near the south bank. Pushing Gabe's stroller, Samantha led the way. A sandy beach allowed them to get right next to the water.

Lifting Gabe onto her hip, she pointed to the ducks paddling about twenty feet from shore. Reaching into her bag of bread crumbs, she tossed a handful into the water to lure the birds closer.

As the ducks drew near, Gabe wiggled and pushed against her. "Down."

She set him on the ground, and he clutched her finger as he danced in glee. He grabbed a handful of bread crumbs and threw them to the ducks. Unfortunately, the crumbs traveled about two feet then fell to the shore.

Gabe's lower lip began to tremble and tears welled in his big blue eyes.

"Poor baby, he's teething." She explained so Alex wouldn't think Gabe was usually this moody. She reached to pick him up again.

"Let me." Alex swept the boy up and deposited him on his shoulders. He handled Gabe with such ease and grace, she knew he'd done this before.

Startled by his new position in life, Gabe grabbed Alex's hair in two chubby fists. Not even flinching, Alex stepped up to the lapping water and offered Gabe another handful of bread.

This time most of the crumbs landed in the water and the ducks swam closer to feed. Delighted, Gabe proceeded to feed the ducks.

Samantha swallowed hard, the sight of father and son together both a pleasure and a pain. This was what she wanted for Gabe, a father who spent time with him. Over the past few months, she'd seen how close the extended Sullivan family was; brothers, cousins and grandmother supported each other without question.

Unconditional love, it was what Samantha desperately wanted for Gabe. But why did it have to be at the cost of her relationship with him?

It wasn't the time or the place, but Samantha had to know. "Would you consider shared custody?"

Alex whipped around to frown at her then he winced as Gabe pulled his hair. Reaching up to ease the boy's grip, Alex was struck by the vulnerability she couldn't hide. He went completely still.

Her creamy-white skin looked bruised under green eyes shadowed by worry. She'd lost weight, too. Her jeans and white cotton sweater clinging to her curves a little less faithfully than the day she'd come to his home.

She looked as if the mountain breeze could lift her up and carry her over the small pond. He wanted nothing more than to hold her and keep her safe, but he couldn't allow sympathy or temptation to sway his better judgment.

He didn't want to hurt her, but he couldn't honor her request. Visitations, yes, but not shared custody.

When he looked back on the years after his parents died, the only thing holding him together while he struggled to help with his brothers had been knowing who he was and where he belonged. Gram worked hard to give his brothers and him that sense of continuity and belonging. No way he could look her in the face and do less for his son.

He hadn't planned on this child, but now that he knew of him, Alex meant to do everything in his power to provide the best home possible for him.

Alex wouldn't put his son through the displacement

that came from splitting a child between shared households.

"I'm sorry, but no."

Defeat momentarily showed in the slumping of her shoulders as she turned away, shielding her disappointment from him. His fingers flexed around Gabe's ankle with the urge to reach out to her. Alex regretted causing her distress, but not even for her would he compromise his beliefs.

Somewhat desperately, she pleaded. "At least tell me you'll get him a dog. To play with and keep him company. I was going to get him a puppy for his birthday."

She probably thought it was a small thing to ask. For him it wasn't small at all. He'd taken on all he could handle for now. "I need peace at the end of the day. Dogs are loud and messy."

"No dog?"

"No dog."

He saw her hands clench into fists and she led with her chin when she swung back to him.

"Why are you doing this? You don't even want children. Everyone knows your marriage ended because your wife wanted children and you didn't."

All sympathy ended under a sudden lash of sorrow and pain. He turned his attention back to the ducks, but still he saw her in his peripheral vision. Indignant. Justified. Wrong.

"No. My marriage ended the day my daughter died."

Chapter Three

Alex heard Samantha's breath catch. And from the corner of his eye, he saw that she went completely white, the color draining from her cheeks.

"My God, Alex. I'm so sorry." Without hesitating, she stepped forward, pressed herself to him and held him close. "What happened?"

He went still, bracing himself against the show of sympathy, against the fresh wave of pain. "I don't talk about it."

"Of course." She took no exception, simply hugged him harder and said again, "I'm sorry."

Her unexpected compassion touched him deeply. Perhaps because she was the first person outside his family and Doug to express sorrow for his loss. Caught in a sudden maelstrom of emotions, he clenched his teeth to contain the constriction in his throat.

Words were impossible. But he wasn't ready to let

her go. He lifted his right arm to hold her close, at the same time reaching for Gabe's foot so he wouldn't slip from his perch on Alex's shoulders. Instead of Gabe's sneaker, Alex's hand closed over Samantha's fingers. Even as she comforted him, she held his son safe.

Something buried inside him clicked into place. Tightening his grip on the two of them, he closed his eyes and quietly mourned the loss of his baby girl, so tiny, so frail she hadn't survived being born three months early.

His six-year marriage hadn't survived the tragedy. He'd been furious when his wife became pregnant against his wishes; but he'd gotten over it, supporting her through her pregnancy, even coming to love the child she carried.

Finding out his baby had died because his wife hadn't followed doctor's orders killed any feelings he had for her. She'd pretended to give up smoking, yet continued behind his back. Then he learned the doctor had advised complete bed rest a month before she went into premature labor. She'd said nothing to him and continued to work, then cried buckets when she miscarried.

He'd cried, too. But not in front of her. He'd cried alone.

No, he hadn't wanted children, but his biggest regret wasn't that his ex-wife deliberately betrayed him by getting pregnant. It was that he never got to hold his daughter in his arms. She came and went without him ever touching her. Without her ever knowing how much her daddy loved her.

His friends and neighbors had known he hadn't wanted children, so his ex got all the sympathy. He was ignored, or worse, treated as if he were relieved. They'd made him feel he had no right to compassion, no right to grieve publicly. So he'd held it all inside.

And promised himself he'd never father another child and risk this pain and loss again.

Samantha pretty much hated his guts because of the custody issue, yet she recognized his pain and offered comfort unconditionally. What an amazing woman. He admired her courage and selflessness. For that reason he revealed more than he normally would.

A cloud moved in front of the sun. The breeze turned chilly in an instant. And Gabe began to wiggle. He hit Alex on the top of the head. "Down man."

Samantha stepped back and looked up, first at him, gently gauging his emotional state, then with a nod and a rueful smile, she moved her gaze up to Gabe.

"What's wrong, little man, did we ignore you? Did the duckies swim away?" She retrieved the bag of bread crumbs from the ground where they'd fallen during the brief embrace and handed Gabe a palmful. "The duckies will come back."

"No duckies!" Gabe threw the bread crumbs down. The crumbs rained around Alex and Samantha, most of them lodging in Alex's dark hair. But not for long. Gabe hit Alex on the head demanding to be let down, sending scratchy crumbs down his shirt collar. "Down man!"

Alex happily complied.

Samantha immediately swooped Gabe up and deposited him in his stroller parked near a picnic table on the grass. "Bad boy." She admonished as she tucked the blankets around his legs. "You don't hit."

"Bad man," Gabe countered, sending Alex a teary-eyed glare. High pink spots heated his cheeks.

"Good daddy," she corrected, "he helped us feed the duckies." Gabe began to cry. Samantha dug out a bottle for him then laid the seat back on the stroller. In seconds Gabe lay quietly sucking, eyes closed.

"Sorry about that." Samantha turned her attention to Alex, swiping at his shoulders and hair to help remove crumbs. "He tires easily when he's teething."

"No harm," Alex assured her. Unless she kept touching him. He could only stand so much petting before his body reacted like the red-blooded man he was.

Soft hands caressing his chest and arms, long fingers running through his hair, the scent of honeysuckle and woman made it hard to think or to consider the other families occupying the park and sports center.

He took one huge step back before reason completely deserted him and he laid her down on the grass right here and now. Bending at the waist, he shook his head in a pretense of getting rid of bread crumbs. In reality he needed the blood back in his head.

Because watching her bend over the stroller, seeing her tend the fussy baby, feeling her hands on his body gave him some fanciful notions. Like maybe taking her home, as well as taking his son.

When he stood up and the idea still held appeal, he realized he had something to consider.

Samantha watched Alex take a seat at the picnic

table. Sighing a mixture of frustration and relief, she joined him. Both of them sat facing the pond. If he hadn't stepped away when he did, she'd have jumped him.

Well, maybe not. Her restraint may have held. But she wouldn't bet money on it. The man was hot. Steaming. And she'd gotten carried away with the feel of those hard muscles, broad shoulders, silky hair… Okay, stop.

She waved a hand in front of her face, pretending to chase off a bug. When had the day turned so warm?

"Have you been married?" he asked suddenly.

"No," she answered, the simple truth her second biggest regret. She wanted nothing more than a loving husband, children and a dog. A real family. Her family. "I was engaged once. It ended when my mother died, and I got custody of Sarah. My fiancé decided he was too young to be the father of a twelve year old."

His eyebrows lifted, and he assessed her from top to bottom and back again, lingering appreciatively on the valley and slopes of her hips and bust. She shifted restlessly, feeling the weight of his gaze as she would a caress.

"Fool." When he returned his attention to her face, desire showed in his eyes, but his voice held disbelief. "You don't look old enough to have been Sarah's guardian. She was twelve, how old were you?"

Samantha took the question as a compliment though Sarah's voluptuous curves always made her appear more mature than she'd actually been.

"I'm thirty-one. I'd just turned nineteen when our mother died."

Behind narrowed eyes she saw him calculating ages and dates. The results hit him hard. "Lord, I'm thirty-six. She was little more than a child."

Samantha shook her head. "Sarah always rushed life as if she couldn't get through it fast enough. She prided herself on looking older, acting older, pretending she was older. She hadn't been a child in a long time."

He looked unconvinced.

"She was twenty-three." Because Samantha knew Sarah wouldn't appreciate the importance being given her age, she defended her sister's choices. And that would be the end of her arguments. "Well beyond the age of consent. There's no need to beat yourself up."

Alex slowly accepted the truth in her words. The woman he remembered had been vibrant and assured. She'd known what she wanted and how to get it. For a couple of days, at a time when he needed it, what she'd wanted had been him.

Or more specifically what he could give her. How ironic he'd been on the island to distract himself from the news that barely a year after their divorce his ex-wife had given her new husband a baby girl. The news had him mourning his daughter all over again. And he'd gone to the island to forget.

Only to be used again.

No, he had nothing to apologize for.

"So you were engaged once." He brought the conversation back to Samantha. "Did you leave anyone special back in Phoenix?"

"Special?" she repeated ruefully. "No. I'd been seeing someone for two years. He lasted six weeks after Gabe came to live with me."

Alex began to see a pattern developing, one that explained a lot. "Samantha, you must have known when you moved to Paradise Pines and introduced Gabe to me there'd be a chance I'd seek custody."

Dropping her gaze from his, she stared out over the pond the weight of the world heavy in her eyes. "I knew," Samantha agreed. "I just never believed it would happen. In my experience men usually have the opposite reaction. My sister Sarah's father left the country after my mom told him she was pregnant. So, no, I never seriously considered the thought of you wanting Gabe."

Over the next three weeks, Social Services appeared several times for surprise visits. Samantha did her best to make a good impression. She locked a smile in place, answered all the questions—no matter how personal—with good grace and maintained friendly chatter for all she was worth.

And as soon as the thin, cheerless woman left, Samantha worried that she'd talked too much, smiled too much, tried too hard.

Alex appeared three more times to visit with Gabe. Samantha cooked dinner for him once, and he took them out once. All very civilized, considering they were at war with each other.

The third time he came around, he took them to

Gram's for Sunday dinner and a birthday celebration for Gabe. Earlier in the day, Samantha had taken Gabe to the pond for a picnic of his favorite foods, ending with cupcakes and a handful of gifts. He'd been excited by the plastic building blocks, but she'd felt let down. She'd wanted to give him a puppy.

The center of attention at Gram's, he officially met all his uncles, except the second-oldest Sullivan. A Lt. Commander in the navy, Brock Sullivan rarely made it home for family events.

Alex's grandmother and his cousin Mattie went out of their way to make Samantha feel comfortable.

"We're so glad you brought Gabe into our lives," Gram said. "I'm sorry for the loss of your sister."

"Thank you. It's very generous of you to have a party for Gabe."

Gram's smile lit up her face. "My pleasure. We haven't had a baby in the family since Ford was in diapers." She chatted on, regaling Samantha with family history.

Samantha found it interesting that Alex's father named his six boys alphabetically to help him keep track, beginning with Alex and ending with Ford. Though the twins Derrick and Everett went by Rick and Rett. Samantha realized her sister had honored the Sullivan tradition by naming her son Gabe.

Though a little overwhelmed at being surrounded by so many Sullivans, Samantha enjoyed the impromptu party. Especially since Gabe thrived under all the masculine attention.

"Time for presents." Mattie began to gather up used cake plates. "Cole, can you bring in the gifts?"

A few minutes later Gabe tore into a pile of gaily wrapped packages. He shrieked and giggled and wanted to stop and play with each new gift. Alex watched from behind the blue Victorian-style sofa, involved but distant.

Finally, Gabe reached the last gift, a box bigger than him. He peeled back the paper, then Ford cut open the box and lifted out a life-sized, stuffed, rocking dog.

"Doggy!" Gabe's eyes grew huge and he immediately climbed on and began rocking.

Alex had bought Gabe a dog.

Samantha met Alex's benevolent gaze across the room and her heart twisted. She didn't know whether to laugh or cry. The whole evening left her feeling torn. Fear and worry at war with love and loyalty.

She loved the welcome the Sullivans were giving Gabe. The fact that Alex had noted and made arrangements to celebrate Gabe's birthday were exactly the actions she'd hoped for in a father when she brought Gabe to California. Yet the same thoughtful actions were what the courts would be assessing in their determination of who gained custody of Gabe.

When she compared her building blocks and cupcakes to Alex's rocking dog and three-layer, double-chocolate birthday cake, she despaired. Because if she were the judge, she knew which way she'd rule.

Alex stood talking with the twins, but watched out of the corner of his eye while Samantha gathered Gabe's gifts into the large empty box. She bent one way then another, making Alex's mouth go dry at the enticing site of her pretty butt. Deliberately, he dragged his gaze away from the temptation she offered, frowning when he spied his brothers Rick and Rett standing together, arms crossed over their chests, enjoying the same view.

The twins ran the family jewelry store, Sullivans'. Rick handled the business end of things while Rett controlled the creative side. Neither encroached on the other's territory, but together they'd made Sullivans' the most prestigious jewelry store in San Diego. Last year, *Now San Diego* magazine had named both men on their top ten eligible bachelors list.

"Hey," Alex demanded their attention. "Go ogle your own women."

The twins lifted their brows in identical expressions of speculation. As a declaration, he couldn't have made his interest clearer if he'd shouted the news through a public address system.

Good. He didn't want any of his brothers getting romantic notions about Samantha. That wouldn't suit his plans at all.

Each of them grabbing an arm, the twins pulled Alex through the archway into the dining room. They ganged up on him one on either side, to begin their questions.

"How long have you had delusional thoughts in that direction?" Rick nodded toward Samantha.

"She's a beautiful woman, what's delusional about that?" Alex meant to stick as close to the truth as possible. He had his reasons for pursuing Samantha, reasons that were nobody's business but his.

But he disliked lying to family. So he'd tell the truth, just not every detail.

"She's your son's aunt." Rick stated the obvious. "And you're looking to take Gabe away from her. She can't be too happy with you."

"She's one hot aunt." Rett offered his opinion, looking at Samantha through the archway as she straightened and brushed golden curls away from her face.

Alex shot his elbow into Rett's gut. "Put your eyes back in your head."

Grinning, Rett rubbed his stomach. "I was just admiring your taste."

"That's not what you were admiring."

"No." Growing sober, Rett tagged Rick with a questioning glance before looking back to Alex. "Are you serious about her?"

"I don't know yet." Alex shrugged. "It's pretty new." Samantha turned, caught them staring. Her cheeks blushed red, and she flicked him a speculative glance before joining the other women. "But it feels right."

As each day passed every moment Samantha had with Gabe grew more precious, until finally their court date arrived. Her attorney, Mr. Keyes, a slender dark-haired man with an exhaustive wit and a clever mind, followed her into the courtroom. Immediately, a representative from Children's Protective Services stepped forward to take Gabe. Mr. Keyes had prepared her for this moment, yet she hugged Gabe to her, reluctant to hand him over to a stranger.

Mr. Keyes cupped her elbow, a silent message to cooperate. Mustering all her strength, Samantha released Gabe. As the heavyset woman walked away with a fussing Gabe, Samantha told herself everything would be okay.

Squaring her shoulders and lifting her chin, she looked around. The room wasn't as big as she'd expected. In fact, it had only three rows of seats on either side of an aisle. Behind a wooden railing a large desk presided over two smaller tables.

"Samantha," Mr. Keyes indicated the table to the left inside the railing, "let's do this."

She nodded and led the way, wishing all the while that he'd been more encouraging about the outcome. He'd warned her to be realistic and prepared her for the fact that the judge would probably rule in the father's favor.

She preferred to be hopeful, to believe the judge would see the merit of leaving Gabe in the custody of the aunt who loved him.

As if on cue, Samantha heard a commotion and glanced over her shoulder to see Alex Sullivan holding the door open for Gram and his cousin Mattie. Two of his brothers, Cole and Ford Sullivan, followed the women into the room.

The show of family support made Samantha feel very alone.

His family filed into the seats behind Alex. Gram smiled gently and nodded at Samantha, sympathy in her vivid Sullivan blue eyes. But she showed her true support as she reached over the railing to pat Alex on the shoulder. The warm gesture denoted togetherness.

The Sullivans defined family love, they were a bois-terous, close-knit clan who respected each other and had fun together.

Truthfully, Samantha envied the sense of belonging they shared.

She looked at Alex and found his steady gaze on her. Deliberately, she looked away. Gabe was hers. If he had any heart at all, the judge had to agree.

Judge McCray settled his glasses more firmly on his prominent nose. "I have before me DNA tests proving Alexander Sullivan is the father of the minor Gabriel Dell. I also have a petition by Alexander Sullivan to have the birth certificate of said minor changed to include his name. And another seeking guardianship and custody. A countersuit has been entered by Samantha Dell."

Hearing the judge outline the petition was worse, much worse than being served with papers. Alex really meant to take Gabe away from her. She'd come to hope, as Alex continued to visit Gabe and the three of them got to know each other better, that Alex would see the merit of shared custody.

The proceedings continued with testimony from social services, child behavioral specialists and character witnesses. Everything Mr. Keyes presented was equaled or bettered by Alex's attorney. Samantha's confidence began to fray.

Foreboding filled her as she felt the weight of Judge McCray's survey before he stated his decree. "The court commends Miss Dell on her sense of responsibility toward her nephew. If she were married, I may have been disinclined to remove the child from a complete home as I feel it's important for a baby to have two parents during his developmental years. However, that's not the case for either petitioner.''

The judge opened a file. ''As stated during testimony, Social Services made several unscheduled visits to the homes of both Mr. Sullivan and Miss Dell. Both homes were found to be adequate. I'm ready to render my decision.''

Samantha's blood chilled. She couldn't breathe as fear clenched her lungs. She just wanted to take Gabe home, to shower him with love and hugs. The judge had to understand. He had to see Gabe belonged with the family he'd known all his life.

''Whereas the father never relinquished his rights to the child, the law is clear.'' Judge McCray's voice drew her attention to the front of the room. ''This court grants custody of the minor to Alexander Sullivan.''

The judge punctuated his decree with a bang of the gavel, shattering Samantha's world.

No! Everything in her screamed in denial. She couldn't move, couldn't think. Devastating loss caused her stomach to churn and weakened her knees. Fighting back tears she forced herself to stand along with everyone else.

She should have run with Gabe when she had the chance.

Maybe it wasn't too late. She sought out Gabe, found him seated on the social worker's lap, his little body tense as he sipped his bottle, his gaze locked on Samantha. Waiting for her to come claim him. For one wild moment, she calculated the odds of making it across the room, grabbing him up and fleeing to safety.

"Samantha, it's over." Mr. Keyes's voice brought her back to sanity.

Feeling nauseous she headed for the door, needing air but needing distance more. A minute. She just needed a minute to pull herself together.

Alex's hand wrapped around her elbow, pulling her to a stop just shy of the door. "I want to talk to you."

"You had no right!" Samantha shook him off. Unable to look at him, she focused on the door and escape.

"He's my son, Samantha." The intensity of his will breathed hot over the back of her neck as he leaned close.

Breathing heavily, she spun and got right back in his face. "He's my blood, too. I'm his family, too."

"Samantha?" Mr. Keyes stepped between her and Alex. "I'll see you home."

She welcomed his intervention yet still hesitated. She wasn't ready to walk away from Gabe even though legally he was supposed to go home with Alex.

Where was Gabe? She watched as the social worker handed him over to Alex's grandmother. Sadness welled within Samantha along with tears. She blinked, but it didn't help.

Alex squared off against the lawyer. "Miss Dell and I are having a conversation."

"That's not what it looked like to me," Mr. Keyes challenged, chin to chin with Alex. "It looked like you were badgering my client."

Alex ignored the other man and spoke directly to Samantha. "I have something important I'd like to discuss with you. Then you can see Gabe."

Snake. Using her nephew to get his way. But it worked. Love for Gabe swayed her. She needed to hold him before they took him away, to feel his small strong body tight against hers.

"I'm all right, Mr. Keyes. Thank you for your help today."

Alex visibly relaxed when the lawyer walked away. He switched his gaze to Mattie and Gram. He nodded toward his grandmother and cousin. "I'll ask them to take Gabe outside. We'll meet them out front in a few minutes."

Simmering with resentment, Samantha watched as everyone followed Alex's direction. Of course she understood his reasoning, but it didn't make watching Gabe being taken away any easier. Involuntarily, she took a step after him.

Once again Alex grasped her elbow, stopping her. She jerked her arm, but he held her easily.

"Hold still," he commanded in a low voice. "You'll see him in a minute."

Poor Gabe, he'd been incredibly good today, so when he looked longingly at Samantha over Gram's shoulder, Samantha summoned a smile, putting all her love in the gesture. She did want what was best for him.

Alex squeezed her arm, whether in approval for her compliance, or to gain her attention she didn't know. And didn't care. As soon as Gabe was out of sight, she put extra effort into freeing herself and this time succeeded.

Holding up his hands in a pacifying manner, Alex gestured for her to precede him. "In here." He held open the door to a small, book-lined room.

Fine, she'd listen to what he had to say then she'd find her lawyer and get Gabe back.

Careful not to touch him, she entered the vacant room and turned to face him. She immediately took a step back, then another. He took up too much space. At six-two, he towered over her five foot four inches even with the added height of her three-inch heels. The stark black suit he wore lent an intimidating line to his broad shoulders, an image helped along by his authoritative stance.

"Okay, I'm here." Samantha stopped her retreat and thrust her chin in the air. If he thought she'd give up without a fight, he could think again. "What do you want?"

Alex indicated a chair. "Have a seat."

"No." She already felt at a disadvantage, sitting would only intensify the feeling.

He frowned, then shrugged as if her standing didn't matter. "I know you're upset, but it's done. And this won't take long."

His arrogance just made her want to fight him more.

Agitated, she paced to the bookcase then back. She flung out her hand in the direction of the parking lot. "I love that boy. I won't give him up."

Alex blocked her path. "Once again you're overreacting. I have no intention of keeping him from you.''

Brought up short, Samantha instinctively retreated a step, distancing herself from his overwhelming presence. ''You don't?''

''No.'' He, too, stepped back, allowing her to breathe easier. He fixed her with an impatient stare. ''If you'd calm down and listen you'd know I mean for you to be a part of our family.''

Slowly, both confused and suspicious, she sat at the table and folded her hands on the wooden surface.

''Okay. I'm calm,'' she said.

Alex strolled to the opposite side of the table and surprised her by sliding into an empty chair. His expression carefully blank, he placed both hands on the oak finish.

''I want you to marry me and help me make a home for Gabe.''

Chapter Four

Samantha stared at Alex, unable to believe her ears, yet unable to stop a wild rush of bittersweet hope. To marry and make a home for Gabe…becoming a family would give her everything she most wanted in life.

There was only one problem. The marriage he proposed didn't include love. Of course it didn't. They were strangers.

Settling back, she tried to relax. Best if she appeared calm, collected, in control. Someone had to bring some sense to this situation. "Are you insane?"

"Why?" Alex carefully kept his emotions hidden behind a bland expression. "Because I want to provide a home for my son?"

"He had a home. With me."

"And now his home is with me. But the judge was right, Gabe needs a mother and a father."

Her knuckles whitened where her hands laced together on the tabletop. Her heartbeat sped as fast as her whirling thoughts. She and Gabe had come so far in the months since he'd been placed in her custody. Yes, they'd had growing pains, but together they'd bonded into a family.

More than ever, Gabe needed constancy. He'd already had to adjust to losing his mother. Now he needed to know he was loved. It would be harder for him if they were kept apart, if he lived in one house and she in another.

"What did you have in mind?" she asked cautiously.

Alex lifted an eyebrow. He'd watched surprise, fear, worry, speculation and finally hope cross Samantha's expressive features. He'd intrigued her. Good. Once the shock of the idea had passed, she'd be more open to reason.

"He's my son, my responsibility. I won't shirk my duty toward him. We are, however, strangers. And as you mentioned yourself, raising a baby is a lot different than educating one."

After years of watching children grow up, first his brothers then his students, Alex absolutely believed providing a balanced family was essential for any child. His visits with Gabe and Samantha had given him the solution. He'd provide the home, his sense of duty demanded that, but his emotions weren't involved, couldn't be involved. Marrying Samantha would complete the family unit Gabe needed.

She'd provide the love.

For Gabe, of course. Alex didn't need or want to complicate his life with messy emotions. He'd tried that once. Never again.

Caring hurt too much.

Opening his heart to another child was not an option. The love dug too deep, the wonder so pervasive it consumed you, and the loss of a part of you made your heart bleed.

No, never again.

He'd watched Samantha work with the kids at the high school, seen her gentleness, humor and the patience she displayed with each student. She was good with kids. And her devotion to Gabe couldn't be questioned.

"Alex," she said, protest tight in her voice. "You and I are the strangers."

"But we're adults, and we're not confused by the events of the day." Strangers? Wrong, not since the first time their eyes met. The chemistry between them was centuries old. Primitive in its power. Potent in its allure. He'd fought it for months. Today he counted on the chemistry working in his favor.

"Speak for yourself. I'm highly confused at the moment." Something—anxiety maybe—flashed in Samantha's eyes before she quickly looked away. A frown marred the delicate line of her forehead.

"Why?" he demanded. "My proposal is straightforward."

She shot to her feet. "Your proposal is crazy."

In direct contrast to her agitation, he calmly relaxed in his seat. Meeting the heat in her gaze with cool purpose, he said, "You get to stay with Gabe, and he gets a home with two parents. Everyone benefits."

"And you, Alex, what do you get out of it?" Arms crossed over her chest, she challenged him.

He smiled, not at all intimidated by her feistiness. In fact, he welcomed it. She'd looked entirely too vulnerable, too alone in the courtroom.

"I get my son." His plan would not work without honesty between them. He watched as her chin lowered a notch. "And I get you."

"Me?" Her gaze never leaving his face, she blinked twice. "You want me?"

"Don't be coy." Standing, he moved around the table. Her surprise couldn't hide her desire or the hope in her eyes. Longing at war with caution. This wasn't the first time he'd seen the intoxicating combination in her sea-green gaze. "You want me, too."

Clearly torn, she swayed toward him then away, as if undecided between meeting him halfway or fleeing in full retreat. He had to give her credit when she stood her ground.

Watching her torture her full lower lip sent raw cravings racing through his blood. His eyes linked with hers as he drew nearer.

"We—" the word came out in a breathy whisper, puckering her lips prettily. He lowered his head. But she planted a hand against his chest, stopping him. Clearing her throat, she tried again. "We shouldn't. It'll only complicate things."

He took her hand, lifted it to his shoulder. "Wrong. It will simplify things." This close, her soft scent inflamed his senses and sent logic out of reach. Circling her waist he achieved full body contact with one forceful jerk. "Nothing short of a nuclear blast will stop me from tasting you."

For all the power in his words, he used care in

claiming her mouth, gently soothing her tender lower lip with soft flicks of his tongue. She tasted sweet, lush, womanly. He wanted more, took more. Angling her head he deepened the kiss and felt his heart lurch.

She went up on her toes to get closer to him, but it wasn't close enough. He lifted her off her feet, swirled his tongue around hers while her arms tightened around his neck and she answered his passion with honest hunger. Sensation twirled them up and away so only the other existed in this space and time.

Past and future had no substance. Only now mattered, and the sheer exquisite meeting of body and soul. She made him forget where they were. Almost.

Her breasts pressed to his chest sent his blood pressure soaring. Now he'd had a taste of her, he never wanted to stop. Which answered one question. They were definitely compatible.

Easing away, he took satisfaction in her unfocused gaze and limp posture. He helped her sit before putting some much-needed space between them. A few feet and a solid table should be enough to keep him from grabbing her again.

"We'll have a short courtship, thirty days tops, followed by a quick wedding. Everyone will assume proximity led to love, and we'll let them."

She blinked, then narrowed her gaze on him. "You want people to believe this is a real marriage?"

He lifted an arrogant eyebrow. "Make no mistake. It will be a real marriage."

Suddenly defensive, she crossed her arms over her chest. "But not a love match."

"We'll be a real family." He understood Samantha's hesitation. She loved her nephew, wanted what was best for him.

Alex believed a marriage between them was for the best. In a strange way they were already a family. Marrying Samantha would simply make it official. His proposal may be impromptu, but it felt right. "You want that for him don't you?"

"Of course, but—"

"Samantha, you've been in education long enough to know a two-parent home is the optimal situation for a child. You said yourself Gabe's been through enough. Marriage is the perfect solution."

"I've been in education long enough to know it's not that simple."

"We both want what's best for him. That's simple." It was Alex's bottom line. He had nothing more persuasive to say.

The fight went out of her, leaving a vulnerability she tried to hide. She surged to her feet. "This is too sudden. I have to have time to think."

Her answer wasn't the one Alex wanted, but he inclined his head in agreement. "Don't take long. The sooner we're married, the sooner Gabe can settle into a sound routine."

And the sooner she'd be in his bed.

A brisk wind blew dead leaves across the courthouse steps. Samantha welcomed the cold, clear air. It helped soothe her frazzled nerves, cool her overheated body. She walked beside Alex but kept a gap of more than a foot between them.

She'd need more space yet before she could think

about his proposal. The man was way too much of a distraction.

Suddenly Samantha heard Gabe crying. Poor baby, he huddled against Alex's grandmother, a pitiful bundle of misery. His little butt poked out in resistance as if he'd fought to escape and that's as far as he'd gotten.

Gram rocked him gently and patted his back, but he continued to cry. When Alex's cousin, Mattie, tried talking to him, he just turned his head.

Samantha's heart broke. She looked to Alex but didn't wait for his nod. She ran to her baby.

Gram greeted her with relief. "Poor little guy wanted his mama," she said as she passed Gabe to Samantha. "He was okay until we stepped outside, then there was no consoling him."

"Mama." Gabe clutched her around the neck and laid his head on her shoulder, his tiny body shuddered once, twice then relaxed against hers.

No words could describe the wonder, love and sadness that swelled her heart.

"I'm sorry he was a bother, Mrs. Sullivan." Samantha rubbed his back in soothing circles. "He's such a good baby, but he can be stubborn when he wants something. And it's been a tough day for him."

"Please, call me Gram," she insisted. More than a smidgen of sympathy reflected in her direct gaze. "It's been a tough day for us all. As for stubbornness, I'm sure you've noticed it runs in the family."

Oh yeah, Samantha noticed.

"Is he okay?" Alex appeared behind Samantha, surrounding her and Gabe with his strength. His right arm circled her waist as he ran his left hand over Gabe's head in the first tender touch she'd seen him make toward his son.

"He'll be fine. He's just upset by all the tension and being passed around a lot."

Alex's grateful glance included both his grandmother and cousin. "Thanks for looking after him for us. I'm sorry he gave you trouble."

"He was a little fretful is all." Gram dismissed the apology. "No trouble."

"Samantha's right, it's been an upsetting day." Mattie put an arm around her grandmother and nodded at Gabe already asleep in Samantha's arms. "It's time we all went home."

"Gabe should go home with Samantha tonight," Alex said.

Surprised, Samantha looked up, suspicious of his motives, but she saw only concern in his eyes. "Are you sure?"

"I trust you, Samantha. You wouldn't have brought him to my attention if you meant to steal him from me."

He'd said much the same the day they'd gone to the pond. His confidence in her revealed a knowledge of her she hadn't guessed he'd possessed. Until now. The thought scared her just a little. And touched her deeply.

"I don't know. I'm pretty mad at you about this whole situation."

He smiled knowingly. "You know how to fix that."

* * *

Samantha pulled a handful of socks from the dryer. As she sorted and folded Gabe's clothes, her mind buzzed. So much had happened today, she didn't know where to start to make sense of it all.

She'd lost Gabe.

And Alex had asked her to marry him.

She didn't know which was more devastating. If she married Alex, she'd be reunited with Gabe, but she'd be married to a stranger.

Well, not exactly a stranger. She knew a lot about Alex. She'd made it her business to learn as much as possible before she trusted him with Gabe. The kids at the school respected him. The teachers and administrative staff nearly worshipped him. The businessmen of the community looked up to him.

Except for hating his guts over the whole custody issue, Samantha plain liked him. He was a decent guy who made no excuses for loving his family. What wasn't to like?

She dug deep into the dryer again, taking comfort in the homey scent of soap and fabric softener as she pulled out the last of the load.

She wished she had a better idea of what Alex's expectations were. The tone he used when speaking of Gabe made her feel Alex's view of the future wasn't real rosy.

Who could blame him? A man who'd suffered the loss of one child and a baby traumatized by another change in caretaker made a volatile mix at best.

Picking up the spray bottle of stain remover, she went to work on Gabe's jeans. A line of rusty red above the knee caught her attention. A smile tugged at the corner of her mouth while tears gathered in her eyes, blurring the colors in front of her. The slightest cut or scrape sent him scurrying in her direction for a Band-Aid and a kiss to make it better.

His unquestioning faith in her to take care of his hurts made her realize the biggest loss she'd suffer because of the judge's decision. Gabe's trust.

Because she wouldn't be there to kiss his boo-boos anymore.

Unless she married Alex.

Tomorrow, after school, he'd be by to pick up Gabe and his things. She'd never dreaded a deadline more in her life. She felt impotent, as if whatever she did, whatever choice she made, someone lost.

If she fought for custody, she'd be depriving Gabe of his father. But if she agreed to marry Alex, she'd be giving up on her dreams for a future of her own with a man who loved her and children they'd create together.

Which brought her back to Alex's proposal.

Closing the lid to the washer, she spun the dial to start the load. Then, leaning against the machine, she rubbed at the ache under her breastbone. She felt as if she'd just talked herself into a corner, with Gabe on one side, Alex on the other, and her longing for a family splitting her down the middle.

In the living room, she set the hamper on the couch and began folding and transferring the clean clothes to Gabe's suitcase.

If she married Alex then she'd get to stay with Gabe, he'd have a home with both a mother and a father, and Alex would have her in his bed. A place she longed to be.

Everyone benefited. Except it was false.

Or was it? Perhaps her presence would provide enough of a buffer between the two that they'd actually forge a relationship despite themselves. Because she had no doubt they were going to clash.

In her opinion, neither of them—man nor boy— was ready to allow someone new into their hearts.

She set the stack of folded clothes on the couch on her way to check on Gabe. He slept peacefully on his back, as always he'd kicked his covers aside. She carefully tucked his blanket under his chin, her heart turning inside out with love for him.

She was going to miss him so much.

Though tempted to wake him just so she could cuddle him, she resisted and tiptoed from the room. She flopped down on the overstuffed brown couch next to Gabe's suitcase and leaned her head back with a sigh. So, she rubbed her throbbing temples, had she just talked herself into accepting Alex's proposal?

Yes. No. Maybe.

If she were convinced the marriage was in Gabe's best interests, she'd do it in a heartbeat. The trouble was she couldn't trust her instincts. She'd dreamed of having a family of her own for so long. It would be so easy to talk herself into accepting, to say intimacy would lead to something more and dazzle herself with hopes of love growing between them.

Then she'd be the one building impossible expectations. Or maybe her expectations were already impossible. Hadn't her relationships with both her fiancé and her ex-boyfriend, Ben, proven her standards were too high? Both men had accused her of putting the children before them, and they'd been right. But if they'd put the kids first once in a while, or even Samantha, the balance wouldn't have been so lopsided.

Or was that her bitterness speaking?

No denying the devastation she'd felt when her fiancé departed. Yes, the two of them had been too young to take on the responsibility of Sarah, but for better or worse meant working together. Love meant sharing the good and the bad and making life easier for each other.

When he left, she'd still been too young. Only then she'd been young and alone. And heartbroken.

Yet she'd managed.

Ben's defection, though less heartrending, left her feeling more alone than ever. Disillusioned again. Her dream out of reach. Again.

She knew she should just give up on her pursuit of unconditional love. She couldn't do it. The reasons why were unclear but had something to do with her father. As if giving up hope would diminish him in some way.

Okay, that did it. She no longer knew if she was making sense.

Because, she groaned, she'd just talked herself out of marrying Alex. At least until she saw how he and Gabe got along.

Enough! For the last two hours her overtired mind had worried at the problem just as her tongue worried at a sore tooth. She needed to think about something else, anything else.

With a sigh she remembered she still had to move Gabe's jeans to the dryer. Then she intended to take a couple of aspirin and go to bed.

Her eyes closed, and, with an effort, she forced them open. In a minute she'd get up and take care of the laundry.

In a minute…she'd get up…

Sleep claimed her.

In her dreams a mouth, hot and slick, moved up her neck to nibble at the sensitive spot just behind her right ear. She bowed her head to the left allowing the mouth better access, then she shivered when sharp teeth bit her earlobe, sending pleasurable pain to her nerve endings.

Desire heated her blood. She wanted more. Just as she'd wanted more earlier today at the courthouse. Was that today? Or yesterday?

Didn't matter, her subconscious warned, enjoy the moment.

But—

"Enjoy…" the whisper was in Alex's deep voice, his mouth brushing her cheek as he uttered the word.

"Yes," she said in surrender as she turned into his arms. She'd known from the first touch of skin on skin that it was Alex who held her, seduced her.

She opened her mouth under his, welcoming him in, meeting and mating, tongue against tongue. Rising on tiptoe, she threaded her hands in his short dark hair, pulling him closer. His hands on her hips, holding her to him, completed the circle binding them together.

Samantha hummed in pleasure. This, yes this, her

man in her arms, was what she needed. Life should always be this simple, this exciting, this right.

Alex slowly lifted his mouth to move in a moist trail down her throat, stopping to lick the curve of her neck and then blow softly, causing her skin to prickle in awareness. She held his head, urging him silently to do it again. He did, adding a nip at the end that made her squirm with longing.

She arched her body into his. How real this seemed.

Alex raised his head, cradled her face in his hands, and said, "Marry me and it could be real."

Samantha jerked awake. She blinked, bringing into focus the well-lit living room. The empty hamper sat at her feet, Gabe's suitcase occupied the couch beside her and his jeans were still damp in the washer.

Alex wasn't here, hadn't been here. The passionate embrace had all been a dream, her subconscious dealing with what her conscious mind refused to face.

She'd purposely kept all thoughts of the kiss they'd shared buried. The decision she faced was difficult enough without remembering the way he tasted, the way he smelled or the way her body fit into the shelter of his.

Well, her subconscious had made itself felt—her body still throbbed from the erotic power of her dream. The question was, what did it all mean?

At seven on Friday morning, weary from lack of sleep, Samantha stood at the sink mixing batter for pancakes. Today, she needed comfort food.

A knock at the front door offered a reprieve from the vicious cycle of indecision her mind had resumed first thing this morning. Wiping her hands on a dish towel, she went to get the door.

Her attorney stood on the doorstep, his hands tucked into the pockets of a black trench coat.

"Mr. Keyes, this is a surprise."

"I wanted to make sure you were all right. You seemed upset when I left you yesterday." He indicated the interior with a nod. "May I come in?"

"Of course." Samantha stepped aside, gesturing in invitation. "Come to the kitchen. I have coffee on and pancakes cooking."

Mr. Keyes breathed deep and made a small sound of approval. "Smells good. But I'll just have a cup of coffee." He settled at the table. "Did Sullivan give you any trouble after I left?"

"No." Samantha got a mug from the cupboard, poured the coffee and set the sugar on the table before moving the griddle to the back burner and joining her visitor at the table. "He asked me to marry him."

Mr. Keyes didn't even blink, and Samantha figured it took a lot to shock an attorney. "That's unexpected."

"You're telling me." She cupped her hands together, leaned forward in earnest. "I need to know the truth. What are my chances of fighting the judge's decision and getting custody of Gabe?"

He met her gaze squarely. "Not good. Sullivan holds all the cards. Besides being the boy's natural father, he's a respected member of his community with strong family ties. In my opinion, the most you can hope for is generous visitation rights. And that's because you've been Gabe's primary caretaker for the last six months.''

He pushed his coffee aside and leaned forward to continue. "He has a very strong sense of family obligation. You told me that when you hired me. My research shows his parents died when he was fourteen. His grandmother was busy putting the family business back together, so he practically raised his brothers. From the moment he confirmed Gabe was his, he's assumed responsibility for him. It's how his mind works.''

Yeah, that's exactly how Alex's mind worked. But his sense of duty didn't relieve her of her responsibility toward Gabe. Neither did it in any way take precedence over her love for her nephew.

"I know how important family is to the Sullivans,'' she said. "It's important to me, too. Gabe is my only family now. That hasn't changed.''

"I should warn you that the longer this drags out the less chance you have.'' After glancing at his watch, he apologized. "I'm sorry, I'm going to have to go.''

Samantha rose to walk with him to the door. "And if I married Alex?'' she asked, fully prepared to face his disapproval.

Keyes shrugged. "Don't expect me to be shocked. Lots of people marry for reasons other than love. Realistically, it betters your position. You gain instant custody, and if the marriage fails, you go before the court as Gabe's mother.''

He stopped on the porch and offered a last piece

of advice. "Find a way to work with Alex, Samantha. It's the only way to gain custody."

Gabe played on the living-room floor, pounding a peg through a wooden block with a plastic hammer. The late-afternoon sun streamed through the window, gilding him in golden light.

His dad was due any minute.

She lifted Gabe onto her lap, kissed his dark curls and swallowed the hard lump in her throat. Tears threatened, but she held them back. She didn't want Gabe to see her sad.

"Mama loves you."

Gabe patted her cheek. "Mama."

The sound of a car door slamming drew her attention. Her time was up. Drawing deep on her reserves of strength, she carried Gabe with her to the front door.

"Daddy's here. And Uncle Cole." She watched as the two men climbed from Cole Sullivan's truck.

Alex wore a collared shirt tucked into blue jeans, making him look bigger and more rugged than usual. Somehow he always appeared taller and broader in casual clothes. He'd brushed his dark hair into perfect order. Overall, he appeared relaxed but in control. The confidence in his blue eyes added to the impression and sent her chin up a notch.

"Hello, Samantha," he said in the same voice he'd used in her dream last night.

Panicked, she turned and led the way inside. She couldn't look him in the face while remembering the sinful things his mouth had done to her, the naughty things she'd wanted to do to him.

"Gabe's things are all packed. Hi, Cole." She greeted Alex's brother as he followed Alex into the house.

Cole, the third youngest of the six Sullivan brothers, stood as tall as Alex and his eyes were just as blue, but Cole's hair was a shade lighter. He owned the local nursery and he carried himself with strength and confidence, his muscles well defined under his shorts and Save The Rain Forest T-shirt. He was gorgeous and easygoing. Unlike his complicated older brother.

"Hey, Samantha." Cole crossed to her side and gave her a chaste kiss on the cheek. "You have everything ready? I brought my truck so we can get it all in one trip. We're going for pizza when we get everything loaded. You in?"

Tears stung Samantha's eyes as she placed Gabe in his playpen. Grateful to Cole for making her feel as if she were a part of the move and not a helpless bystander, she gave him a small smile before reaching for the first box.

"Sure," she said, her voice a little husky. "I'm always up for pizza."

"I'll take that." Alex suddenly stood on the other side of the box, so close the back of her fingers brushed his chest. Even that casual touch affected her pulse rate.

"Okay." She thrust the box into his hands and backed up a step.

He didn't immediately move away. Reluctantly,

she met his gaze. From the compelling expression in his eyes she realized he was the one behind Cole's invitation.

"I'm glad you decided to come with us," he said. Then, hoisting the box to his shoulder, he grabbed a suitcase in his other hand and headed out the door.

Darn, somehow it had been easier to accept the invitation when it came from Cole. Too late to back out now. Besides she had to think dinner together would help ease the transition for Gabe.

Pulling up the handle on Gabe's second suitcase, she rolled it down the walk to the driveway. On his way back inside, Alex hesitated beside her, his gaze flickering to the large case.

She arched a brow at him. "It rolls. I think I can handle it."

He nodded but spoiled his acceptance by saying, "I'll be back in a minute. Don't try to lift it into the truck."

She rolled her eyes heavenward, truly uncertain if he was being macho or simply old-fashioned. Probably the latter. He was too confident to worry about being macho, but knowing Gram he'd have been raised to show proper respect and manners.

She guessed she shouldn't fault him, and she didn't, not really. But he needed to realize she was a strong capable woman who would fight for what was hers.

At the truck, she lowered the handle then lifted the heavy case. The effort strained her muscles, but she managed to heave the suitcase up onto the tailgate then push it into the truck.

Satisfied, she turned to find both Sullivan men bearing down on her, both frowning heavily. She simply grinned, dusted her hands together and started for the house. ''What's next?''

As she passed Alex she met his direct blue gaze and knew he'd gotten the message. Never underestimate the power of a determined woman.

Chapter Five

They drove to El Cajon for the pizza. Gabe rode in his new car seat between the two men in the truck and Samantha followed in her car. Alex held the door as Samantha carried Gabe inside. The scents of tomato and garlic made her mouth water. She'd been too preoccupied to eat earlier, and she suddenly realized she was starved.

The restaurant catered to the rowdy crowd. Loud, reasonable, with good food and fast service the place packed in the people. This Friday night a boys' soccer team celebrating a successful game added to the crush.

Still, Samantha's party was soon seated in a booth, Samantha and Alex on one side, Cole on the other, and Gabe in a high chair on the end. She sent Alex a sidelong look, letting him know she'd noticed how smoothly he'd managed the seating arrangements.

He responded by taking up more than his share of

the bench, spreading his arms and legs so he touched her from shoulder to shin. She tried to scoot over but there was nowhere to go. He'd effectively trapped her between his body and the wall.

"I want sausage and black olive," Cole said without opening the menu.

Gabe drummed the tray in front of him, his head swiveling this way and that as he took in the action around him.

Cole stood. "Come on, kid, I've got quarters. I'll let you ride the pony." Cole winked at Samantha before strolling away, Gabe tucked on one hip.

As soon as the pair disappeared into the crowd, the waitress stopped at their table. Alex ordered two large sausage and black olive pizzas and three sodas. When they were alone again, he turned to her. "Word is, a strange man was seen leaving your house near dawn this morning."

Caught off guard, she swung to face him. "Excuse me?"

Alex propped an elbow on the table. "Three people stopped by my office to tell me of your early-morning visitor."

He didn't seem overly worried by the news. Which meant what? That he didn't care? Or that he trusted her? After the way he kissed her yesterday, she found it hard to believe he didn't care. She sat back in her seat and laced her fingers together.

"I see. And you want to know who it was." She nodded, feigning understanding. "Okay. Help me out. Are we talking about the tall dark-haired man or the short dark-haired babe?"

His eyes narrowed. "You've been busy."

Tempted to string him along a little, she decided she'd better keep things as straightforward as possible between them.

"The short guy keeps me busy most mornings. As you'll soon find out. Which reminds me, I spoke to Emily, Gabe's day-care sitter. She'll continue to take him if you want, but if you're going to find alternative care, she needs to know soon."

He nodded. "Thanks. For now I think it's best to keep Gabe's routine as familiar as possible." Alex kept his gaze fixed on hers. "And the tall dark-haired man?"

So he did care. The thought held enough appeal to have Samantha smiling.

"My lawyer stopped by to see me."

"What did he want?"

Was it her imagination or did the tension in his shoulders ease even as a frown drew his dark eyebrows together? Enjoying his discomfort—because honestly until she accepted his proposal what she did and who she did it with were none of his business—she rocked back in her seat.

"Mr. Keyes wanted to make sure you hadn't harassed me. I told him on the contrary, you had proposed."

His shoulders snapped taut again. "Was that necessary?"

"For me, yes. But don't worry, he was on your side." Realizing she held him captive, she hit him with a few questions. "Mr. Keyes told me your parents died when you were fourteen and you helped your grandmother raise your brothers. Is that true?''

His gaze went black as pitch. He made no effort to dissemble though he obviously resented her asking. ''Yes.''

''How could you seek custody of Gabe? You must know how it would feel if someone had taken them away from you?''

He faced forward, avoiding her to take a sip of the soda the waitress had set in front of him. ''I don't have to explain myself to you.''

''I think you do.'' In her need to know she placed her hand on his arm, felt his heat and muscles. She pulled until he turned to her again. ''I got my heart torn out in that courtroom yesterday. I have a right to know why.''

''You know why.''

Her back teeth ground together in frustration. ''Because he's your son.''

''Yes.''

''Damn it, Alex, that's not good enough. If all you wanted was to assuage a sense of duty, you could have paid child support. You didn't have to take him from me, I'd have respected your role in his life.''

A shrug lifted his broad shoulders. ''That's not how my family works.''

''I've seen how your family rallies together. They'd support any decision you made.''

He turned on her, emotion ripe in his eyes. ''Some decisions they shouldn't have to support. There's no way I could look my grandmother in the eye and tell her I didn't want to raise my own son.''

Geez. How did she fight that revealing sentiment? Especially when she thought of Mrs. Sullivan, petite and white haired, who smelled of Chantilly and face powder and smiled encouragingly across a courtroom aisle.

"She must know you didn't want children," she said, half in protest, half in sympathy.

"We never discussed it. But it wouldn't matter. There's a difference between electing not to have children and denying a child you've conceived." His expression became resigned. "You want an explanation. My parents traveled a lot when we were growing up. They died in an earthquake in South America. Gram took us in, kept us all together and saved the family business from my father's neglect. I'm sorry you were hurt, but I'd do anything not to disappoint her. Anything to make sure another child of mine didn't suffer because of lack of action on my part."

Right. He didn't have to dot the *I*s or cross the *T*s. Gram couldn't save the business and mind the family at the same time, which meant the responsibility for his brothers fell to Alex. Samantha didn't need her minor in psychology to recognize he'd suffered from oldest-child burnout or to realize he blamed himself for his daughter's premature demise. The one explained why he didn't want children, the other why he needed to take control now that he had a son.

Glancing across the room to where Gabe bounced and giggled on a faded plastic pony, she knew she couldn't let the conversation end there. "And Gabe?"

Catching her chin on a crooked finger, Alex turned her gaze back to him. Absently, he tucked a loose tendril of hair behind her ear, the brush of his fingers gentle against her skin. "He and I have some getting acquainted to do."

Worry puckered her eyebrows together. "Please have patience with him. He needs to be loved. He's very fragile right now. He just got used to me."

"If you're so concerned about what happens in my house, you know what you can do." His voice held a note of finality. Then he leaned close until his breath washed over her temple. "Have you thought about my proposal?"

She'd like to tell him no, to pretend her every thought hadn't revolved around him for the last twenty-four hours, unfortunately she'd never been that good an actress. "I'm still thinking."

A sensual smile tilted up one corner of his mouth. "Perhaps you need more persuading." His husky tone suggested what form his influence would take.

The heat spiraling through her body tempted her to vacillate just so she could feel his mouth against her for real. Last night's dream had left her unfulfilled. Given half a chance, Alex would take care of that problem.

At a price.

She understood the unspoken terms. Marriage or nothing. Gabe's presence demanded no less from them.

"No, thank you." She politely declined his sensual offer. Looking at him from under her lashes, she ruefully admitted, "I don't think I could survive another dose of your persuasion."

Desire smoldered in the depths of his blue eyes as he moved his gaze from hers to her lips then back again. "Too bad."

Alex insisted Samantha follow them to his place to help settle Gabe. The closer she came to his two-story three-bedroom cabin on the east side of Paradise Pines the heavier her heart grew. Regardless of Alex's insistence, she should have said goodbye at the restaurant and made a clean break.

But she couldn't leave Gabe until she had to.

Cole parked in the driveway next to Alex's sedan, and Samantha pulled to a stop in front then joined the men by the truck.

"You were right," Alex told her, "Gabe fell asleep on the way here."

She forced a smile. "Happens every time. I'll carry him in while you guys get his gear."

He nodded, reaching into the back for a suitcase. "Lead the way."

With the ease of practice, she quickly released Gabe from his seat and snuggled him against her chest. He stirred then settled his head on her shoulder and went back to sleep. She climbed the stairs to the deck behind the two men. Cole dropped his load in the living room then headed back outside while Alex continued down the hall.

"Gabe's room is through here." Alex indicated the first room to the left. "My room is upstairs." He held the door for her, dropping the suitcase next to an oak dresser.

Samantha carried Gabe to the matching oak crib

against the far wall. She viewed the full-scale nursery with mixed feelings, both impressed and dismayed by the show of Alex's commitment to raising his son.

He even had a rocking chair in front of the window.

"The room looks nice."

"Gram and Mattie raided Gram's attic. Some of these pieces have been in the Sullivan family for generations."

"So you slept in this crib?" she asked, contrarily pleased by the continuity of the tradition.

"Me and all my brothers." He indicated a cradle with the name Sullivan carved into the wood. "My father and grandfather slept in that."

"Has your family always lived in Paradise Pines?" She knew the answer, that he'd grown up here. With Gabe's future at stake she'd made it a point to learn as much about Alex and the Sullivans as possible.

Now she wanted to learn about Alex from Alex.

"For four generations," he said absently, as if all families were so close to their roots.

Cole arrived carrying two boxes he set inside the door. "That's the last of the stuff from the truck. If you don't need anything else tonight, I'm going to take off."

Alex clapped his brother on the shoulder. "Thanks for your help."

"No problem. See you, Samantha." With a wave Cole took his leave.

While Alex checked out the boxes, Samantha changed Gabe's wet diaper. Exhausted from his night out, he slept right through the process. She left him in his T-shirt and, knowing he often kicked off his covers, slipped a sleeper on over it.

The whole procedure took about five minutes. She longed to cuddle the baby, but settled for a kiss on his cheek before settling him in his new bed. Then she simply stood watching him, not yet ready to walk away.

She was glad he had roots, that he now had a grandmother and uncles to support and nurture him. Her mother's parents had died before she was born, and she barely remembered her father's parents. They'd lived on the east coast so she hadn't seen them often. Her impressions were of a frail, elderly couple who hadn't quite known what to do with an active six year old.

Lucky for Gabe, Samantha suspected Gram would be a hands-on grandma.

Alex crowded behind her, laying his larger hands over hers on the crib railing. "He'll be okay."

Spice and powder, the scents of man and baby surrounded her in a blend of heat and innocence, seducing her with the need for both.

"I know." Emotion clogged her throat, making the words a whisper.

He rested his chin against the hair at her temple so they touched head to toe. "Don't worry, we'll work something out."

"I know," she said but no sound made it past the constriction in her throat. His reassurances touched her deeply. She leaned into him and nodded, her hair brushing his chin and catching on the bristles of his evening beard.

So strong, so self-assured, so capable she longed for nothing more than to turn into his arms and let him take care of her as well as Gabe. Only knowing she'd be sacrificing her most secret desire kept her from surrendering.

After another moment of watching Gabe's peaceful slumber, Alex kissed her on the top of the head. "Come on, I'll walk you to your car."

Reluctant but resigned, she allowed him to lead her from the house. He held her door while she settled in the driver's seat. Then he bent through the open door and closed his lips over hers in a mind-numbing kiss.

When he pulled away all she could do was blink. Over the pounding of her blood and the racing of her heart she barely heard him say, "Think about my proposal."

From a dead sleep Alex shot straight up in bed.

The baby alarm was going off.

Throwing back the covers, he grabbed the flannel bottoms he wore around the house in the winter, glancing at the clock as he pulled them on. Three o'clock.

He headed downstairs to the nursery at a clip. When he entered the room, the cow-jumping-over-the-moon night-light revealed Gabe standing in his new crib. His small fists were wrapped around two bars, his tearstained face squeezed between the bars as if he was trying to escape.

When he saw Alex, Gabe stopped crying to stare suspiciously. "Man."

"Hey, slugger, what do you need? Your diaper changed? A bottle?"

"Mama." Gabe plopped down on his butt and began to cry again, deep wrenching sobs.

"You'll feel better when you're dry." Alex scooped the kid up and carried him to the changing table. Gabe fought him the whole way, pushing against Alex's chest and demanding Samantha.

"Mama, mama," he pleaded.

"Sorry, kid, it's just you and me."

He wanted Gabe to feel welcome and comfortable in his new home, but Alex believed discipline and routine were necessary in raising a child. Kids pushed against boundaries, it helped them to know where they stood.

"No man. Mama." From the look on Gabe's face, he didn't appreciate Alex's part in the scheme of things. He did more than push. The boy kicked and shoved, twisted and turned, mooning Alex. Twice. And he screamed, loud enough for Alex's neighbors to suspect him of murder.

Finally, holding Gabe down with one hand, Alex got the diaper in place and the tapes tacked down. Thank God for modern conveniences.

In a challenge of wills Alex knew he had the advantage.

He had double master's degrees in education and child development, he'd taught thirteen years in the classroom and he dealt daily with discipline issues at the high-school level.

But this wasn't a matter of Gabe being stubborn. His distress came from confusion with his unfamiliar surroundings and from fear of being with an unfamiliar man. When Gabe called him "man" it wasn't because he thought Alex was "The Man," it was because he didn't know Alex from Jack.

Gabe wanted his mama, and Alex didn't blame him, he wished Samantha were here, too.

"Ma-ma." Gabe hiccuped and his little body shuddered. With his favorite stuffed bunny, Mr. Hops, under his arm, Gabe settled down on the trip to the kitchen and while Alex fixed him a bottle, but when Alex laid him back in his crib, Gabe erupted into a frenzy.

He threw his bottle out of the bed and crawled into the corner. Nothing Alex did would console the child. Alex tried rocking him, walking him and, in desperation, he even tried singing to him. Gabe only cried louder.

Frustrated, Alex nearly joined him.

So much for discipline and routine. After two hours of dealing with the fussy baby, Alex would have given his left arm for a few minutes peace.

Exhaustion eventually wore the little guy down and as the sun began to rise on the horizon, Gabe finally cried himself to sleep.

Hardly daring to breathe, Alex tucked the blanket around Gabe and Mr. Hops. So much for his son's first night under his roof.

Chapter Six

Samantha didn't sleep much Friday or Saturday night. She gave up trying early Sunday when the pink flush of dawn began to lighten the sky. She made coffee, then wrapped a blanket around her shoulders, walked out on the front stoop and sat on the step to watch the new day bloom.

Behind her, the house felt lonely. Every little sound echoed with emptiness.

Funny how quickly she'd become accustomed to having Gabe in her life. How fast she'd developed the instincts of a mother. Only when he was no longer hers to worry about did she realize how strong those instincts had grown to be.

She remembered the day he was born, the day he came home from the hospital, the day she'd held him at his mother's funeral.

There'd been no question, not one, that Samantha would take Gabe to live with her. The two of them had created a family, alone in the world except for each other.

Then she'd found out about Alex.

The sun suddenly broke over the trees, its rays falling across the yard, lighting on drops of dew that glistened like diamonds in the green grass. The inspiring beauty of the scene struck Samantha with unexpected hope.

A new day meant a new beginning.

She needed to face facts. She didn't have to lose Gabe; in fact, she could never lose Gabe. He lived in her heart, if not in her house, but he could be in both. All she had to do was marry Alex.

Fighting Alex for custody served no purpose when both of them should be there for Gabe. She'd given up a lot to bring the two together. So she needed to stop thinking of Gabe with Alex as a bad thing.

But she wasn't convinced marriage to Alex was the answer.

The Sullivans were a large supportive family. Gabe couldn't be in better hands. And it wasn't as if she was abandoning him. Best if she married someone she loved and provided Gabe with some cousins. More family for both of them.

She was considering the possibility of getting a dog when a dark blue car pulled into the driveway and parked. Rather than get out, the driver laid his head back and closed his eyes.

Curious, Samantha hiked the blanket up around her shoulders and went to check why Alex sat in her driveway at six-thirty in the morning on a Sunday. And to find out where Gabe was.

The second answer came before the first. Bundled up in a fleece sleeper Gabe slept peacefully in his car seat in the back. In the front, Alex looked exhausted, his black lashes rested against dark circles under his eyes, his skin pale in contrast. Though he looked relaxed, his shoulders were tense and his forehead was furrowed in a frown.

Uh oh. Something hadn't gone right last night.

Samantha knocked on the driver's window. Alex jumped, stared at her through the glass, then rolled down his window.

"Hey," he said softly.

"Hey. You want to come in?"

He adjusted the rearview mirror to check on Gabe in the back. "No. He's asleep. I don't want to move him and risk waking him."

"You can join me on the step. We can watch the car from there." She opened his door. "I'll get you a cup of coffee."

Leaving him on the stoop, she went inside and came back with two mugs of steaming coffee. "So what's up?"

"Kid doesn't sleep. He doesn't sleep, I don't sleep."

"He was like that right after his mother died. He settled down once we got used to each other."

Hope sprang into his blue eyes. "How long did it take, a couple of days?"

"A couple of weeks. Well, actually closer to a couple of months before he slept through the night."

Alex groaned. "I can't keep driving around in the

middle of the night and at the crack of dawn. You have to marry me. It's the only answer.''

She bit back a smile. He'd been so sure of himself, she'd known he'd face some disillusionment. She hadn't expected him to admit it so soon. Obviously, sleep deprivation made people do strange things. Tenderly, she tucked his hair behind his ear, soothing him with a few strokes of her hand. ''What happened?''

He lifted one shoulder then let it drop in a half-hearted shrug. ''Nothing.''

Ah. Nothing always meant something. ''Did he pee on your silk robe?'' she asked, knowing how outrageous it sounded. Offering a ridiculous suggestion helped put the real problem into perspective, and made it a little easier to talk about.

''No.'' He sent her a reproachful look. ''He peed on my cotton robe.''

''Man, that's unforgivable.'' She responded in mock fury. ''We better tell the judge right now that you won't be treated that way.''

Her mention of the judge made him frown. Weary, he scrubbed both hands over his face. ''There's no going back now. And I wouldn't if I could. But I feel helpless when he won't sleep because I can't get him to stop screaming. Or when he refuses to eat then cries himself to sleep.'' He shot her a hopeful glance. ''Please tell me it gets easier.''

She wouldn't lie to him no matter how down he sounded. ''Yes, and no.'' She bumped his shoulder with hers. ''Don't take it so hard. These things take time. And I'll help. I know I've been fighting you, but I've done a lot of thinking the last couple of days. I've put some things into perspective.''

''And you've decided to marry me?'' he asked as if it was the height of reasonableness, but also as if he was already resigned to the inevitability of being rejected.

Decision time. Wishing she were better prepared for this conversation, she patted his back. Hoping through touch to reassure him of her support even as she rejected his proposal.

''No.''

He looked at her, his eyes intent. ''Why not?''

''Um, well.'' Unnerved by the force of his concentrated gaze, Samantha stalled. She drew in a calming breath. ''Because marriage isn't something I can be practical about. I love Gabe. I will always be available for him if he needs me. But I also want a family of my own some day.''

''Gabe and I can be your family,'' he persisted.

Honestly, the man had the tenacity of a bulldog.

''I'm talking about love and having children of my own. I'm pretty sure that's not what you have in mind.'' Why did her refusal seem to hurt her more than it did him?

He averted his eyes and shrugged. ''No. I can give you passion and fidelity, and promise neither you or Gabe will ever want for anything.''

She studied his profile, noted the lines of weariness around his eyes and mouth. Not for a moment did she doubt his sincerity. He was a good man trying to do what he thought best in an unfamiliar situation.

''And if what I want is another child?''

The cool look he turned on her was answer enough. He couldn't give her everything she wanted.

Knowing she'd made the right decision, but feeling curiously deflated, Samantha left Alex to his brooding to check on Gabe in the car. He was awake, waiting with great patience in his car seat for someone to come claim him. When he saw Samantha, his little body vibrated with excitement. He kicked his feet and held out his arms, demanding she pick him up.

"How's my big boy? You're a happy guy, aren't you?"

"Mama." He wiggled and bounced in her arms, a smile lighting his whole face. Then he proceeded to lecture her. He framed her face with his pudgy little hands and babbled at length, telling her of his displeasure. She knew this by his references to the "man" and the "bad man."

She kissed Gabe, encouraging his chatter with the occasional response of, "Is that so?" or, "You don't say?" and, "You're such a brave boy."

Alex grimaced as she walked by him into the house.

She winked and invited him inside for pancakes. While she visited with Gabe in the kitchen, Alex stretched out on the couch in the living room. When she called him to breakfast a few minutes later and got no response, she dropped some Cheerios on Gabe's high-chair tray and went to investigate.

She found Alex, all six feet two inches of him, overlapping both ends of her couch, the cotton throw twisted around his waist. He lay on his side facing out, one broad shoulder wedged awkwardly into the corner.

He looked entirely uncomfortable. Poor Alex, these last few days had been as hard on him as on Gabe.

Wanting to make him more comfortable, she nudged off his shoes and tried to reposition the constricting blanket.

He groaned, rolling onto his back and almost over the edge of the couch. Samantha jumped forward and put her knees against his side to keep him from falling. She tried to roll him back into place but couldn't budge him.

She shook his shoulder. "Wake up. You're going to fall."

One blue eye opened then the other. Then they both closed again. He groaned and half turned to face the back of the couch. His right arm caught her behind the knees and threw her off balance. She landed between him and the couch cushions.

"Morning, Samantha." He wrapped her in his arms and snuggled his face against the curve of her neck. The stubble of his beard scraped softly over her skin.

"Alex." The scent of him surrounded her. He surrounded her. She tried to wiggle free, but he held her too tightly. "Let me up."

No response. In fact, he'd fallen back to sleep. She pushed again, harder, and still got nowhere. Except hot and bothered. Every time she pushed against his chest, she touched heated male muscle. Even through his shirt she felt the hard, hair-roughened skin.

"Alex, you need to let go now." She couldn't stay this way. Gabe was alone in the kitchen. And the longer she lay here, the more she wanted to cuddle close to Alex's warmth.

"Make love with me." His sleep-husky voice sounded close to her ear.

She blinked once, then again, fighting off the desire rushing through her. Her breasts tingled and an emptiness bloomed in her lower body. For the first time in her life she experienced a full-body blush.

Samantha felt both flattered and trapped. She wanted him, too, but it wouldn't be fair, or wise, to succumb to temptation after rejecting his proposal.

When his mouth began to nibble the sensitive skin behind her ear, she dug an elbow into the cushions and tried to rise. "I have to go. Gabe is alone in the kitchen."

"Samantha, give us a chance." His eyes, open and alert now, stayed steady on hers.

"I can't." She stopped struggling and went very still. "Please let me up."

For a moment his arm tightened around her, holding her beside him, then respecting her wishes, he released her.

In a flash, she scurried to her feet and straightened her clothes and hair. She glanced at him from the corner of her eye, finding it easier to look at the dark curls in the open collar of his shirt than the regret in his eyes.

"It's best if we just forget this happened."

He sat up, his long legs sprawled in front of him. "That should be easy," he said in a low growl, "since nothing happened."

Understanding his frustration, she brushed a loose curl out of her face. "Take a nap. I'll watch Gabe."

Alex slumped back on the couch and closed his eyes. "Wake me when you're ready to get married."

Just after nine o'clock on Monday Samantha answered her cell phone on the third ring. "Hello."

"Samantha, it's Emily." Gabe's day-care sitter identified herself, sending alarm skittering down Samantha's spine. Emily, a short Hispanic woman with flawless skin and nerves of steel, never called during the day.

A baby's cry sounded in the background.

Fear caused the breath to catch in Samantha's throat. "What's wrong? Is Gabe all right?"

"He's not hurt, but I can't get him to settle down. He hasn't stopped crying since Alex dropped him off two hours ago. He won't take a bottle. He won't eat. I thought he might cry himself to sleep and feel better when he woke up, but he won't sleep. I think he's hysterical."

"Poor Gabe." Samantha's heart wrenched to hear of his suffering. Worse, his pitiful cries came clearly through the phone. "He's having trouble adapting to the change. He kept Alex up all weekend."

"I called Alex but he's at an event in downtown San Diego. He didn't think he could get here in less than an hour. Can you come get Gabe?" Emily asked, stress evident in her voice. "I wouldn't bother you, but the other kids are becoming distressed."

"Of course I'll come, but I can't take him without Alex's permission."

Emily sighed in relief. "That's not a problem. Alex listed you as a contact in case of an emergency. Can you come now?"

Alex listed her as Gabe's emergency contact? Samantha didn't know what to think. This show of confidence demonstrated his acceptance in a way nothing else could. That he hadn't even told her made the gesture all the more touching, as if he'd considered it a given and so should she.

Samantha assured Emily she'd get there as fast as possible. She notified the office personnel and school district she had a family emergency and fretted every second of the thirty minutes it took to get from Julian to Paradise Pines.

She didn't breathe easy until she held Gabe in her arms. Tears filled her eyes as she gathered him against her bosom. He clung to her, his little body shaking from fatigue. He felt slight as if he'd lost weight. With all his crying, he'd definitely lost fluids.

Intellectually, she knew she delayed his adjustment every time she came to the rescue, but her soft heart refused to let him suffer. So maybe she needed to stop rescuing him on the short term and be there for him every day.

When Emily offered him his bottle, he grabbed it and lay back in Samantha's arms, sucking strongly. She cradled him close, watching as his eyes closed, feeling him grow heavier as he fell instantly asleep.

"Look at that, he's already asleep," she whispered to Emily.

"Poor little guy's miserable," Emily replied. "I expected him to settle down once he recognized the familiar surroundings, but nothing calmed him."

"I'm so sorry for the trouble he caused you."

"Don't be. I just wish I could have done something for him."

Starting to feel the strain of Gabe's deadweight, Samantha thanked Emily for her help and carried Gabe out to the car. Just as she got him settled in his car seat, still asleep and still holding tight to his bottle, Alex pulled into the spot beside her.

In an instant he stood next to her. "I got here as fast as I could." Clearly concerned he peered in the back window at Gabe. "How is he?"

"Sleeping now, but he was screaming when I got here. Alex, we have to do something. He's obviously distraught. And he's making himself ill."

"Drive to my house. We'll talk there."

Alex insisted on carrying Gabe inside to his bed. Samantha followed, making sure Gabe settled in okay. He opened his eyes when Alex laid him in his crib. Gabe frowned when he saw Alex. Seeing the scream building, Samantha moved forward with his bottle and a soft pat on the tummy.

He smiled at her around the nipple, sighed and closed his eyes. Her heart swelled to overflowing, torn between love and regret.

Pushing gently against Alex, she indicated they should leave.

In the kitchen, Alex nodded at a cupboard above the microwave. "Mugs are in there. I'll start the coffee." He filled the pot with water, poured it into the coffeemaker and pushed the brew button.

Samantha carried two mugs to a breakfast nook where an atrium window brought the forest indoors. "I like your house," she said, both because it was true and because she wanted to put off their conversation about Gabe.

On the drive from Emily's, she'd made the momentous decision to marry Alex. Seeing how her presence calmed Gabe simply validated her choice. The problem was she didn't quite know how to broach the subject. She slid into a seat, watching him fill the mugs.

He finally settled into a chair across from her. His gaze caught hers. "So why don't you move in?"

Her blood began to hum. She blushed, suddenly finding it hard to blurt out her acceptance of his proposal. It seemed so cold-blooded. But she reminded herself they'd be marrying for practical purposes not for love.

He filled the silence. "I've tried everything I know to do. I'm at the end of my rope here." His gruff admission echoed his weariness and frustration.

Bracing herself against the anxious flutters in her stomach, she took the biggest step of her life.

"All right, I'll marry you." There she'd said it. She

sighed in relief and waited for Alex to take over from here.

Alex didn't react at all. Seconds ticked by but he didn't say anything. His expression didn't change, not even to blink. After a minute, she wondered if he was breathing, but the steady rise and fall of his chest reassured her.

The total absence of response caused a sick feeling to grow in her stomach. Had she made a fool of herself? He'd just asked her to move in, but had he changed his mind about marriage?

She swallowed to relieve the tightness in her throat. "If you still want to, that is."

With one arm he swept the mugs to the side. Then his eyes locked with hers, he reached across the table, took her face in his hands and, drawing her up to meet him halfway, plastered his mouth to hers.

That quickly, his passion consumed her, carrying her to a place where only the two of them existed. Where skin became so sensitive the soft brush of a lover's breath caused nerve endings to tingle and blood to surge. Where tasting also included touching, and the other three senses exploded through her system.

She clung to his shoulders yet craved to be closer, only the table between them prevented her from wrapping herself completely around him.

He pulled back, continuing to cradle her face in the palms of his hands. Dazed, she wondered at the combination of satisfaction and wanting she saw on his face. She curled her hands around his wrists, knowing her expression revealed the same paradox.

"Oh yeah," he assured her as if his actions hadn't already spelled out his feelings, "I still want you."

"You still want to marry me?" she managed to whisper.

His expression hardened to reflect grim determination. "It's the only way." Shifting his attention to her mouth, he ran his thumb over her lower lip then met her gaze again. "And the sooner the better."

He walked around the table and pulled her into his arms. For one long minute he devastated her senses with mouth, hands and body. When he released her, she found it hard to stand on her own. He braced her until she found her balance.

She licked her lips and held up a restraining hand when he reached for her again. "I have one condition."

His chin went up and he crossed his arms over his chest. "What kind of condition?"

"We wait to make love until after we're married."

His dark eyebrows snapped together and a cold glint replaced the heat in his eyes. "Why?"

She narrowed her eyes, letting him know she didn't appreciate his tone or attitude regarding a simple request. The fact that she, too, felt frustrated saved him from a piece of her mind.

"Gabe's not the only one who needs time to adjust."

"We're not playing make-believe here, Samantha. We will be a real family."

''All the more reason for us to get to know each other better.'' Sighing, she decided to give it to him in terms he'd understand. ''I'm not currently on birth control. I'll be seeing my doctor this week.''

He turned away, ran a hand through his hair, then over the back of his neck. She bit her lip, waiting for his response. Finally, he turned back to her with resignation in his gaze.

He nodded once. ''I accept your condition. So, what are you doing this Saturday?''

Chapter Seven

Since Alex and Samantha had both cleared their schedules, they decided to turn the day into a celebration. Remembering the conversation in the doctor's office, Alex had plans to head for the marina.

The phone rang as they were preparing to walk out the door.

"Hello, dear." Gram's concern came clearly through the phone line. "I heard you had to pick up Gabe early from Emily's. Is everything okay?"

"Actually, Samantha picked him up. She helped me settle him down for a nap. He slept for a couple of hours, and he's feeling better now." Alex glossed over the more traumatic events. To distract Gram, he mentioned their planned trip to the marina.

Gram promptly invited herself along. "It'll be a nice way to become better acquainted with Samantha."

So much for a romantic day on the bay. Instead of

a quiet outing where he got to know Gabe better and touch Samantha often, Alex found himself chaperoned by his grandmother.

Once on the water, his mood picked up. It was a beautiful day for a ride on his twenty-two-foot cabin cruiser. The sun was high, the water blue and the wind mild. He couldn't ask for a more perfect day to be on the water.

Perfect, too, was Gram taking Gabe inside the cabin out of the sun, leaving Alex alone with Samantha. He glanced to where she lay on her stomach on a blanket in the bow of the boat. A long-sleeved shirt covered her upper body, but her long lovely legs, displayed to advantage in blue shorts, were exposed to the slow burn of the sun.

Alex frowned. In San Diego it was never smart to underestimate the power of the sun. The comfortable temperatures often fooled people into thinking they were safe, but even in February they could suffer the effects of sunburn if they weren't careful.

Alex didn't want to see Samantha's soft skin damaged by the elements. After setting the controls and dropping anchor, he grabbed his bag, pulled out the sunblock and sat down on the blanket beside her.

She looked up with a smile and propped herself up on her elbows. "Hello." She kicked her calves in the air, crossed them at the ankle. "Why aren't you driving the boat?"

Leaning down on his elbow, he put himself on level with her, nearly mouth to mouth. "I'd rather sit with you."

Her gaze roved over his chest and shoulders. Lazily, she blinked. ''What about Gram and Gabe?''

''Gram's lying down with him inside. The fresh air and sun have made them both sleepy.'' Alex lifted an eyebrow at Samantha. ''It's just you and me and the seagulls.''

Pink dusted her cheeks. She tried to appear unaffected by his teasing but her eyes failed to meet his. ''Thank you for bringing us out today. It's fantastic. I almost feel guilty for playing hooky.''

''Ahh,'' he said as if he understood completely. Then he leaned closer to breathe against her ear. ''Liar.''

She laughed and knocked his shoulder with hers. ''I said almost.''

He showed her the tube in his hand. ''You need some sunblock or you'll burn.''

She nodded and made to roll over, but he stopped her with a hand in the small of her back. ''I'll put it on. Just lie there and let me take care of you.''

Sitting up, he squeezed a good amount into his palm, rubbed his hands together and began applying the protective lotion to her left leg. Using long, even strokes, he rubbed over her supple muscles. Up, up he went, past the sensitive skin behind her knees. He heard her breath catch, yet he continued to massage up the length of her thigh until his fingers brushed beneath the hem of her shorts. She shivered and the muscles in her legs tensed.

She gasped and sent him a warning look over her shoulder. ''Watch it.''

''Sorry,'' he said, not in the least repentant as he

switched his attention to her other leg. Before he finished, he'd wrung two more breathy gasps from her. Those needy little noises she couldn't quite hide made the blood pound through his veins.

"All set." He slapped her on the tush, deciding he better stop before he embarrassed himself. He rolled away to lean on his elbows and contemplate the ocean.

A light breeze lifted the hair off his forehead, offsetting the heat of the day. But not the heat of touching Samantha. Grabbing his shirt in the back, he pulled it off over his head. He rolled onto his stomach, laid his head on his arms and closed his eyes.

He hadn't had a moment's peace all day, certainly not since Samantha agreed to marry him. She'd surprised him this morning with her change of mind. She was a smart sensitive woman fully capable of seeing sense. And she loved her nephew.

Heaven knew they needed her. One weekend under his roof and his son was sleep-deprived, dehydrated and half-starved. What better proof did she need that father and son needed her to ease the way?

So why this sense of letdown? Why did getting what he wanted, what he'd planned on, leave him feeling dissatisfied?

Not because *he'd* changed *his* mind. If anything, this weekend's experience with Gabe made him more determined than ever to bring Samantha into his home. He needed her help.

Because the thought of being a single parent scared him to death.

Still, the dissatisfaction lingered.

A dollop of cool lotion hit the small of his back. He jerked up, but Samantha's hand on his shoulder pushed him back down.

"We wouldn't want you to burn, would we?" she asked too sweetly. "Just lie there and let me take care of you."

Her care meant more than layering on lotion. Her fingers were strong, digging deep into his muscles nearly wringing a moan from him as she worked on the kinks and knots in his back. What she did to him wasn't decent and shouldn't be allowed in public. But he was too weak to stop her.

He could only endure. And enjoy.

Payback had never been so sweet. Leaning low over him, her breath blew over his heated skin causing him to shiver. Enough was enough. Rolling over, he caught her hands in his. "Stop. Or our engagement will leap from budding to consummated in one afternoon."

On her knees beside him she glowed with satisfaction. "I trust your restraint."

"I don't." He kept hold of her hands not trusting her to keep them to herself. "Behave yourself."

"You didn't."

"Next time I will."

"Gee, I hope not."

He laughed, enchanted by her honesty. "Okay, next time I won't."

"Gram disapproves," Samantha said. She sat across from Alex on Tuesday night in a restaurant on San Diego's beautiful harbor. Lights from the downtown high-rises filled the skyline and reflected off the water like diamonds twinkling on black glass.

Music, a rift of saxophone from the band in the bar, floated on the air, adding a sensual beat to the atmosphere. Scents, sweet from the roses decorating the table and savory from the chicken breast in cream sauce, heightened senses already on edge from Alex's presence.

"Gram's a romantic," he said dismissively, slicing his steak with a deft flick of his wrist. "She'll come around after ten years or so."

"Don't make fun," she objected, upset by Gram's concern regarding their plans. "This could change everything."

Alex froze, a bite poised halfway to his mouth, and sent her a look of disbelief. "How?"

"I don't know." She waved her hand in agitation. "But she's an important part of your family. We can't just ignore her objections."

He bit into his meat, chewed slowly, swallowed with a marked movement of his Adam's apple, all the while watching her closely. "We already agreed to marry. Are you saying you've changed your mind?"

"No, of course not." She was afraid of making another mistake. She didn't want Gabe to suffer because she'd made a bad decision. "But I don't want to cause a rift in your family, either."

"That's not possible." Alex reached across the table to slip his fingers under hers and run his thumb in a caress over her knuckles. "Believe me. In my family we may not always agree, but we always support each other. Gram doesn't disapprove of you or of us getting married. She just doesn't like how fast it's happening.''

That did sound like Gram. Samantha was a bit unnerved herself. Smiling a bit sheepishly, she showed her appreciation for his understanding by squeezing his fingers. ''So I'm overreacting?''

He held up his free hand indicating an inch of space between finger and thumb. ''Just a little.''

Responding to his calm control, she relaxed. ''I guess I'm a little paranoid where Gabe's concerned.''

''Your heart's in the right place so it's okay.'' Lifting her hand, he leaned forward to press a kiss to her fingers. ''Things will get easier once we're married. Now finish your dinner. There's a place I want to show you when we're done here.''

He charmed her every time he kissed her hand, the gesture was just old-fashioned enough to be romantic and just intimate enough to be thrilling. But he nearly stole her heart with his patient encouragement and gentle humor.

''What do you want to show me?'' she asked.

He lifted his wineglass toasting her, his eyes full of promise. ''You'll see.''

He took her to Sullivans'. The family jewelry store had been located in downtown San Diego for more than sixty years.

At eight-thirty, in the Gaslamp District, activity abounded. Tourists strolled the streets, visiting the clubs. Numerous restaurants spilled people, laughing and talking, onto the street, adding to the quiet buzz filling the air.

Some stores were still open, taking advantage of the night traffic. But not Sullivans'. Alex drew out a key ring, deactivated the alarm, then opened the decorative wrought-iron gate and security door. Next he punched in a number on a second alarm. After ushering her inside, he closed and relocked the door.

"Welcome to Sullivans'." He waved his hand, inviting her to look around.

The scent of freshly cut flowers floated soft on the air from exotic arrangements set on pedestals flanking the door. She inhaled deeply as she absorbed the quiet elegance of the store. The paintings caught her attention first, three ocean scenes vibrant with color. Samantha recognized them as Langston's, a local artist who'd gained national acclaim.

Light reflected from every corner of the room as display cases of glass, crystal and gold gleamed in the light cast by a chandelier. Her heels clicked on the black-and-white marble floors as she moved across the room. Busts and other jewelry props in black or white velvet filled the glass display cases, empty now of jewels.

"Very nice," she said. "I bet it's stunning when all the cases are full."

"I don't know much about gems, that's Rett's thing, and Rick's I guess, but, yeah, it's pretty impressive when the place is all decked out."

"Your brothers own the store?"

"No, my great-great-grandfather founded Sullivans' over ninety years ago. Now each of us grandchildren owns a share of the stores, this one, the one in La Jolla and the one opening on Rodeo Drive later this year.''

''Rodeo Drive. Wow, I'm impressed.''

''Rett and Rick are the heart and soul of Sullivans'. Rett's the designer, Rick the businessman, together they've made Sullivans' the number-one independently owned jewelry store in San Diego.'' Pride for his brothers' accomplishments sounded in Alex's voice as he led the way to a door behind a counter.

He used another key, disarmed another alarm, being careful to relock and reactivate each behind them once he'd flipped on the lights. They were in a hallway with two doors leading off both sides.

Everything seemed so quiet, so secure, she felt out of place, like a thief touring Fort Knox. ''Are you sure it's okay to be here?''

He grinned and took her hand to lead her to the first door on the right. ''I'm sure. Rett gave me the current combination this morning.''

When the heavy metal door opened, the lights came on, reflecting off rows of narrow black metal drawers. Stepping inside he led her to the table in the middle of the room and held a chair for her to be seated.

She sank weakly onto the cushions. ''Alex, why are we here?''

''We're here,'' he said, as he went to the left wall and began pulling open the drawers until he found what he was looking for. With a grunt of satisfaction he finally pulled a long slim drawer from the wall and set it on the table. ''To choose your bridal rings.''

Diamonds, rubies, sapphires, emeralds, pearls and

more sparkled in a rainbow of faceted glory. Every conceivable choice of precious gemstones glistened before her, each more beautiful than the next, all beyond anything she'd ever seen.

He sat down across from her. "Pick one."

Overwhelmed she simply stared, unable to focus on any one ring when all were so extravagant. "Alex," she managed to breathe. "I can't accept this."

"I didn't know what you liked." He simply overrode her objections. "So I asked Rett to set aside a variety of different styles and gems."

Awed by the display, Samantha sat shaking her head. She couldn't accept any of these rings. They were...too much. And too little.

Too much in value because, being part owner aside, any one of these rings easily equaled a quarter of Alex's annual salary. Even if their engagement were true and not just a practical arrangement, she couldn't let him spend so much on her.

Too little because with no emotion to back up the giving, his gesture became an extravagance, a waste. Every time she looked at the symbol on her finger, she'd be reminded of how she'd agreed to settle for less than her dream.

She clasped her hands in her lap and looked hopelessly at Alex. "Aren't there any plain gold bands?"

He leaned back in his chair, his expression carefully unreadable. He spoke gently. "What's wrong, Samantha? You have too much style and good taste for these not to appeal to you, so what's the problem?"

Again she glanced over the rows of rings, from stark to fanciful, from bold to subtle, from flashy to classy they were all special in their own way. And if one, a marquise diamond surrounded by a wave of baguettes on one side and round starburst diamonds on the other, caught her attention, it didn't change how she felt.

"I don't want a ring from you, Alex. It's not necessary. Especially in our situation."

His eyebrows lowered in displeasure, but he answered calmly. "Our situation is we're getting married. Exchanging rings is customary."

"Don't be obtuse." For some reason his composure upset her. "You know our circumstances are different."

Anger flashed in his eyes. His tone, however, remained reasonable. "Why? Because we're being practical rather than emotional? Does that mean you're going to be less committed to our marriage? That you're not going to try to make it work?"

"Yes. No. I don't know." Why did he have to make this so hard? "You're confusing me."

He placed both arms on the table, leaning so close he stared straight into her eyes revealing the implacable determination in his. "Let me make it easy for you. Everything about this marriage is real. Not make-believe or pretend. Real. The commitment, the fidelity, the vows."

"Vows to love, honor and cherish," she protested.

"Is that what's bothering you?" he asked. "Don't be fooled. Love dies. We're far better going into this marriage with our eyes open and our goals set."

"You think that makes it real? You think that's enough to make it work?" She heard the note of pleading in her voice but didn't care. Any reassurance he could give her she appreciated.

"Yes, I do," he asserted, his belief showing in the confidence of his expression and posture. "We have more than lust holding us together. We have a purpose. Both of us want to provide a good home for Gabe. It only helps that we're hot for each other."

They were that. So hot, steam practically rose whenever they touched. Which was often. Alex, she'd found, was a toucher. She should have known since his family hugged every chance they got. He made no secret of his desire for her. She still experienced a thrill every time he held her hand in public, or he sat pressed against her side in a restaurant booth.

Yes, she wanted to marry him, she hadn't changed her mind. Still a plain gold band would be fine. She started to tell him so, but he continued with his argument.

"A lot of marriages don't make it, not even after six years." He paused for a moment, a frown of concentration pulling his eyebrows together. "My first marriage didn't."

Six years? His announcement surprised Samantha, sent the thought of rings clear out of her head. She'd had no idea his first marriage lasted so long.

"The loss of your daughter must have been devastating for both of you," she said softly, encouraging him to continue.

"Yes, but it was more than that. We wanted different things in life."

"Oh." Not many details there. And not very con-fidence inspiring, either. She hesitated to ask further questions as he'd been so reluctant to speak of his first marriage, but she decided she needed to know. She couldn't learn from the past if she didn't know about it. "What kinds of different things did you want?"

He pulled back a little, lifted a negligent shoulder then let it drop. He'd opened the door to his past but now seemed reluctant to step through. Shifting his attention to the tray of rings, he answered. "Little things mostly, and some bigger things. She wanted kids. I didn't. She thought with time I'd change my mind. When I didn't, she deliberately went behind my back. But she was my wife, pregnant with my child. Of course I supported her. And I fell in love with my baby the first time I saw an ultrasound."

"Alex." Torn by his confession, remembering his pain when he told her of losing his daughter, she reached out to him, covering his left hand with hers. "She got pregnant, then lost the baby?"

His hand fisted under her touch. "My daughter was born premature at six months. I went as often as I could, but I didn't make it to every doctor's appoint-ment with my wife. I missed the one where he told her the baby was experiencing some distress. He rec-ommended complete bed rest. She cut back on her work hours, but didn't quit."

"Why not? Why take a chance with her child's life?" How could a woman who'd gone to such lengths to get pregnant risk her baby.

He sneered his disgust. "She needed a place to

smoke. I asked her to quit smoking as soon as I found out she was pregnant, encouraged her to get into a program if it would help. Even offered to go with her so she wouldn't have to go alone. She told me she did. She lied. She was still smoking at work. Her selfishness put us both through hell. She destroyed everything that had ever been good between us.

"My daughter existed only long enough for me to fall in love, and then she was gone."

"I'm so sorry," she said, knowing the words were woefully inadequate.

He turned his hand over and curled his fingers around hers. "I've put it behind me. But you'll understand why I trust concrete goals over emotion. I want you to have one of these rings as my promise to make this marriage work."

"Alex." Samantha didn't know what to say. He obviously hadn't put his pain very far behind him.

His effort to share his past touched her as much as his pledge for the future. Yet she couldn't accept such a generous gesture. The money might not matter to him, but it mattered to her. She wouldn't take more than she could give.

Looking longingly at the rows of rings, at the marquise surrounded by smaller diamonds, she regretfully shook her head. "These are too much. I don't need anything this extravagant to know you're sincere in wanting to do what's best for Gabe. I just want a simple gold band."

"Money isn't an issue." For the first time he sounded irritated. But he quickly evened his tone as he went on, "And this isn't about Gabe. It's between you and me. A plain gold band is fine, but,'' he pulled the tray closer with his free hand and went unerringly for the marquise diamond ring, ''you would look better in diamonds.''

With those words he slipped the ring on her finger. It fit perfectly.

Her resolve melted along with her heart. How could she say no when he made it personal? To refuse now would be to reject him. Something she had no desire to do. On any level.

So she lifted her hand to admire the shine and glitter, then shot him a pleased glance out of the corner of her eye. ''It does look good.''

He grinned, a rare occurrence, and lifted her hand to kiss her fingers, his eyes never leaving hers. ''It'll look better with a wedding band next to it.''

Chapter Eight

Nearly a week later, Samantha rushed toward the school gym. She had a date to meet Alex in—she pushed back her jacket cuff to check her watch—five minutes. Perfect. Just enough time to locate Alex and Gabe and get settled before the basketball game started.

She hoped Alex dressed Gabe in his fleece sleeper. The crisp pine-scented air felt good to her, but would be too cool for the baby. She'd found February in Paradise Pines got downright icy.

Hard to believe a week had passed since she agreed to marry Alex. Time had taken on a whole new dimension, real time and Sullivan time.

In order to ease Gabe into his new schedule, she spent every evening with father and son, and each morning she picked Gabe up and dropped him off at Emily's. Alex did his share, insisting on putting Gabe to bed and picking him up from day care. Gabe remained leery of Alex and vice versa, but each day the two became a little more accustomed to each other.

Just as she and Alex were becoming better acquainted each night after Gabe went to sleep. Talk about quality time. She knew his taste in books and music better than she knew her own.

And she just plain knew his taste. Pure male, potent and addictive. Hard to resist. She took care to escape before things went too far, though each successive night became a more advanced lesson in control.

When they were together, reality blended with practicality until the reasons for their engagement blurred and the physical closeness took on the appearance of emotional commitment. Alone in bed at night she lectured herself on keeping her head in order to protect her heart. Because, though the lines blurred for her, she had no doubt Alex saw them just fine.

Rushing as she was, she almost stumbled over him before she saw him. He sat on a concrete bench off the path of the traffic coming and going between the parking lot and the gym. She'd come from her office inside the school or she wouldn't have encountered him.

He sat with a young cheerleader. The sound of her crying reached Samantha on the cold night air.

As she watched, Alex handed the girl his handkerchief. With a muffled sob she buried her face in the white square. Alex talked softly to her, too softly for Samantha to hear. Whatever words he used, they seemed to be getting through to the girl. Her cries began to ease and her shoulders stopped hitching.

Most men fell apart at the first sign of tears. Not Alex, he saw beneath the surface to the underlying pain. His insightful authority allowed him to be stern but fair. Which in turn made the students feel they could talk to him. He was a good principal.

Too bad he couldn't bring some of that closeness home with him. He still held Gabe at an emotional distance. He interacted with the boy, but he never let his guard down.

Alex continued to talk to the girl, his voice taking on a lighter tone, and Samantha heard a girlish giggle. After a couple of minutes, the cheerleader thrust his handkerchief back at him and ran into the gym.

Samantha strolled forward and took the girl's seat on the bench.

"Hey," he greeted her with a strained smile. "Where'd you come from? And why didn't you get here five minutes ago?"

"My office," she answered. "And I did, but I didn't want to interrupt. What happened?"

"I'm not really sure. Something about dropped batons, first dates and a dog named Queenie." He ran a hand through his hair. "She ran past me as I was headed into the gym, she was so upset I had to follow."

"Of course." She bumped her shoulder against his, telling him she knew he couldn't not follow.

"I didn't understand half of what she said. Thank God. I told her a story of a boy I went to school with whose shorts got caught on another player's watch during a basketball game. He had his pants ripped off in front of the whole school.''

''And she laughed at that?''

This time he bumped her shoulder. ''She's a teenage girl. A guy loses his pants, of course she laughs.''

''The story made her feel better.''

''That, and I told her how the boy came out for the second half of the game in new shorts to face the crowd. And later that year he was valedictorian.''

Suddenly suspicious, she leaned forward to see his face better in the shadowy light. ''Was the boy you?''

Rather than answer, he stood and pulled her to her feet. ''Come on, the game has probably started. Gabe's inside with Coach Anderson.''

His evasion just made her more sure of her guess. She tugged at the hand she held. ''It was you, wasn't it?''

Fighting an indulgent smile, he shook his head at her persistence. ''My brother Rick, but don't tell him I told you, or he'll hurt me.''

She laughed as he meant her to, but when he turned toward the gym and the light fell on his features, she saw the weariness stamped in the lines of his face. Even after a long day he'd taken the time to comfort a distressed girl. He was such a good man he made her heart ache.

The shrill sound of a whistle followed by the squawk of a buzzer announced the start of the game.

''We better go.'' Alex drew her forward, but she resisted.

Instead she stepped back, leading him into the shadows. She circled his neck, pulled his head down and pressed a kiss to his lips. "That's for being such a nice man."

"Nice?" His lip lifted in disdain. "I sit through ten minutes of waterworks and all I get is *nice?* You can do better than that."

He sealed his mouth to hers, deepening the kiss. The demanding pressure of his mouth caused her to shiver. She arched into him, seeking more of the delicious sensations he sent thrumming through her blood. He made her feel alive, cherished, hungry. Wanting more she threaded her hands in his silky hair.

Oh yes, this was better than nice. This was off-the-scale fabulous.

He lifted his head and hers fell back on her neck like a rag doll. He'd stolen her strength, making her limp. In another time and place, she'd knock him to the ground and steal it back.

"Okay, I give. You're a bad, bad man."

"We have to stop," he said, his breath moist against her skin as his mouth moved over her neck.

"Why?" She kissed his jaw, rasping his beard with her tongue. "We're engaged."

"Yeah." He moved his lips back to hers, kissing her once more, hard enough to last. Then he lifted his head, placed a hand in the small of her back and led her toward the light. "But we're not married."

Still swirling from the amorous interlude, Samantha tried to catch her breath. Realizing she'd just had her condition thrown in her face, she sighed. "You're not just bad, you're mean."

* * *

Thursday night Samantha returned late from a professional meeting in San Diego so she skipped going to Alex's. She missed her guys but figured this time alone was good for them. It was after eight when the ping of the microwave announced her dinner was done. She opened the door and reached in to pull the TV dinner out. Steam burned her. Sucking on her singed finger, she grabbed a pot holder with her free hand.

The spaghetti smelled good, fragrant with spices and tomatoes. Unfortunately, when she peeled back the cardboard cover, the watery noodles and flattened lumps of red sauce didn't look as appetizing as they smelled.

She could hardly believe only two weeks had passed since the judge gave Alex custody of Gabe. Despite how upset she'd been following the court's decision, she felt good about how things were going.

According to Alex, Gabe slept through the night last night, which was the best news she'd had since the judge made his decree. The way Gabe had settled down this week had reinforced the rightness of her decision to marry Alex.

Taking her first bite of spaghetti, she thought about her upcoming wedding. When Alex proposed, he'd mentioned a short courtship and a brief engagement.

So far, he'd been the one to set the pace, so presumably he had a particular time frame in mind. He'd been joking about last Saturday. Thank goodness. Tomorrow she'd ask him. She needed to start making plans if he intended to marry soon.

She poked at the soggy noodles, disappointed in

the meal. With a sigh she pushed the half-eaten spaghetti aside. She didn't need a large wedding, she didn't need elaborate, she didn't even require formal. If she couldn't have romantic, she'd be satisfied with intimate and elegant.

The truth was she didn't know what she wanted, or more accurately what she could allow herself to want. The little girl in her, the adolescent dreamer and the woman ready for love, all those hidden parts of her longed for the moment of glory they'd secretly dreamed of forever.

A knock sounded on the front door followed immediately by the doorbell. She'd heard a car a moment ago, but she hadn't paid much attention. After setting her dishes in the sink, she went to answer the demanding summons.

Looking through the peephole, she saw Alex standing on her step. Her eyebrows shot nearly to her hairline. As she watched, he stretched his neck and tugged at the collar of his shirt. But his nervousness didn't cause her surprise. His attire did.

He wore a tuxedo. Complete with a bow tie and cummerbund. In his arms he carried red roses and a heart-shaped velvet-covered box of candy. Behind him a limousine idled in the street.

She swung the door open. "Hello, handsome."

He smiled, visibly relaxing as his blue gaze ran over her face and then the jeans and a baby-blue crop-top sweater she'd changed into after work, lingering for a moment on the strip of bare skin between waistband and hem.

"Hi, beautiful. These are for you."

"They're lovely." Samantha accepted the flowers and candy, carefully balancing both in her arms. She stepped back and led him to the living room. "Aren't you a day early for Valentine's?" She nodded at the waiting limousine. "Is someone stealing you away? Do you have to break our date for tomorrow?"

He shook his head. "These are not for Valentine's Day." He cleared his throat. "They're for my bride. Will you marry me, Samantha?"

Her chest tightened as his proposal spoke straight to her heart. How had he known she needed to hear those exact words? Practicality aside, a woman still wanted to be asked. His proposal a week and a half ago had been more a demand than a question.

Still, being asked here and now confused her. "I've already said I will."

"I know. I'm glad." He gestured toward the window and the limousine in the street, his motions unusually jerky. "I'm talking about now. Will you run away with me to Las Vegas and be my bride?"

He wanted to elope? For a moment, shock held Samantha silent, not because the idea didn't hold appeal, because it did. But the spur-of-the-moment action wasn't Alex's style. She set the flowers down on the coffee table then turned back to Alex, who had ruined the line of his tux by shoving his hands in the pants pockets.

Needing the contact as much as he looked as if he did, she walked over and wrapped her arms around his waist. "Are you sure you want to do this? What about your family? What about work?"

His arms immediately surrounded her, holding her close. He might have appeared edgy, but he felt rock solid. And when he lifted her chin on one finger to cover her lips with his, he demonstrated his usual masterful control.

She had to force her eyes open when he raised his head. He looked steadily into her eyes, but his voice held a note of huskiness when he spoke. "I arranged for us to have tomorrow off, so we'll have three days. Gabe is in the car. The rest of my family is waiting to be picked up once you say the word."

Ah, so this spontaneous moment was more planned out than she'd thought. Now that sounded more like Alex.

She rose on tiptoe, caught his lower lip between her teeth, then said against his mouth, "What are we waiting for?"

"Not a damn thing." He hauled her tighter. "I can't wait to make you mine."

In truth she couldn't wait for him to be hers. "I need five minutes. Will you clean up the kitchen while I throw some things in a bag?"

He nodded. "But don't worry about bringing much. We'll pick up most of what we need for the wedding in Vegas." His mouth connected with hers in a hard hot kiss before he released her and stepped back. His blue eyes held a provocative gleam. "And after the wedding, you won't need anything."

"No. Okay. Fine." Shaking off the devastating impact of his appeal, she straightened her spine. "Right. I'll pack light."

* * *

The six-hour trip from Paradise Pines to Las Vegas passed in a blur. As soon as the limousine turned onto the freeway, Gram declared the start of Samantha's bridal shower. Her protests that a shower wasn't necessary and didn't fit with the spirit of an elopement were blatantly ignored.

"Nonsense, dear, it's our elopement," Gram declared. "We can do what we want. Because it's spur of the moment doesn't mean we can't observe all the traditions. Mattie's brought a few games, then we have presents and cake."

A family elopement. And they'd brought along cake.

Samantha shouldn't have been surprised. The Sullivans always went full out for family. Catching Alex's gaze across the length of the car, she silently apologized for leaving him alone. He smiled and winked, encouraging her to have fun.

Accepting a glass of champagne, she decided to go with the flow. Time and miles flew by. Samantha laughed at suggestive jokes, blushed over risqué games and giggled over naughty stories all in hushed tones so the men and Gabe couldn't hear. Gram's frank and earthy input surprised Samantha. Sometimes outright shocked her. She'd never laughed so hard in her life. She felt like a teenager again, sharing secrets with her best friends.

A few feet away the men were having their own party, drinking champagne—a bottle for Gabe—tossing around jokes, talking sports while a basketball game played on the in-car TV. Because of Gabe they were much tamer than the women but seemed to be having a good time.

They made a loud and boisterous group, divided but together. And every minute of every mile Samantha's awareness of Alex grew. She often felt the sensual weight of his gaze, and, skin tingling, she'd look up and meet his eyes. Blue eyes lambent with hunger, his features drawn tight with anticipation.

His expression turned her on more than all the jokes and stories put together.

Need, both physical and emotional, hit her hard, like an arrow to the heart. She actually reeled back in her seat and breathed easier for the distance between them. Wrong place and time for the physical. Wrong relationship for the emotional.

Or was it? She accepted a refill of champagne and decided to let herself feel. She'd committed herself to this man, to this marriage; she'd be cheating them both if she gave less than her all to the success of the relationship.

As someone thrust a gift-wrapped package into her lap, she lifted her glass in a silent toast to the future. No more holding back.

Alex sipped champagne and watched his lovely bride-to-be open a present from the small pile stacked beside her. The giggles from the women had changed to oohs and aahs as they exclaimed over the contents of the gaily wrapped packages. Samantha refused to hold the contents up, simply passing the box between the women to see.

A sense of satisfaction settled in Alex. Everything was going just as planned. After tomorrow, Samantha would be his wife. She'd be in his bed and in his house. Taking care of him, taking care of Gabe. Allowing Alex the distance from Gabe he needed to protect his heart.

He'd already come to care too much. Mentally he was hooked. When he looked at Gabe, every protective nerve in Alex went on high alert. He'd lay down his life for the boy without hesitation. But emotionally a primal instinct stronger than his will resisted all attempts to open his heart.

He'd learned, too well, the lesson of a parent's vulnerability to loss. No matter what he did to keep his child safe, he was still subject to the capriciousness of fate.

Alex didn't do helplessness well. And he never wanted to do that kind of pain again. So he'd do his duty and pray the emotion would follow.

In the meantime, the sooner Samantha moved in, the better.

"Oh, my." The reverent tone drew Alex's attention to Samantha. The last box from the pile rested in Samantha's lap. Her eyes sparkled as she fingered something buried in a ream of pink tissue paper. A pretty rush of color brightened her cheeks as she turned to hug Mattie.

The box shifted and a spill of white fell to the floor. Samantha quickly snatched up the white confection of satin and lace.

But not before he had time to picture her in the sheer piece of fluff.

Embarrassed she looked around to see if anyone had noticed. When her gaze connected with his, he lifted his champagne flute and toasted her, letting her know he anticipated the moment when she'd be wearing the tiny scrap of lingerie.

At his gesture a new light of desire came into her eyes and a small smile lifted the end of her pretty bow lips.

The trip suddenly seemed endless. Despite the comfort and conveniences, he wanted to be there, in Las Vegas, in front of the altar, saying his vows in the presence of his family, God and Elvis. He wanted the wedding over and the honeymoon to begin.

He wanted Samantha all to himself. In a hotel suite. With a Do Not Disturb sign on the doorknob.

And if he continued with that line of thought, he'd embarrass himself in front of his grandmother.

However, he didn't have to deny himself completely. Crooking a finger, he beckoned Samantha to join him. She'd just taken a bite of cake, and she chewed slowly while she contemplated his demand. Then she tantalized him by deliberately running her tongue along her upper lip.

Little tease. He repeated the action, beckoning to her then patting the seat beside him.

This time she responded. She should have looked silly walking to him on her knees, carefully balancing her plate of cake. With the glint of Eve in her eyes she appeared seductive rather than frivolous. Finally, she reached him and he helped her to the seat beside him.

Looking at him through her lashes, she said, "Hi."

"You're pretty pleased with yourself." He gathered a crumb of cake from her upper lip then ate the crumb from his finger. "How's the cake?"

''Delicious.'' Her tongue flicked out at the corner of her mouth to soothe the skin where his finger had touched. ''Want a bite?''

Yeah, he wanted a bite, of her. She looked so happy he didn't have the heart to tell her he'd already turned down cake. Instead, he opened his mouth and let her feed him.

She watched him chew, the humor slowly leaving her features to be replaced by an odd intensity. Her teeth gnawed at her lower lip. The sight of her torturing the plump moist flesh pushed him over the edge. He lowered his head and covered her mouth with his.

She tasted sweet, a combination of icing and her own unique flavor. He deepened the kiss, swirling his tongue around hers and gently suckling. She shuddered in his arms, and his body responded.

Somehow he marshaled his control and lifted his head. It took her a moment to compose herself. Finally, lazily, she opened her eyes and focused on him.

He leaned close to whisper in her ear. ''Are you having fun?''

A smile broke across her face, and she made no effort to contain her joy. ''I am. Thank you for everything. This has been amazing.''

He smoothed the line of her cheek with a gentle stroke of his thumb. He liked seeing the happiness in her eyes. She worried too much, about Gabe, about him, about the future. Watching her over the past few weeks, he'd seen how much she cared, how hard she worked to make everyone happy, often at her own expense. He wanted to ease her worries and protect her from the harsh reality of not being able to please everybody all of the time.

She deserved more than she was getting from their arrangement, but selfishly he intended to hold her to it. Gabe needed her. So did Alex, more now than when he first proposed.

And not just for Gabe's sake.

Which should scare the pants off him. The Lord knew her influence already invaded every aspect of life. He might even care if her presence didn't make everything run smoother, taste better, smell sweeter. Feel softer.

So he enjoyed her company. So he appreciated having someone to talk to who understood what he dealt with on a daily basis. So he liked sharing a joke, an idea, a chore. It didn't mean he was getting soft on her.

It just meant he'd made a good deal.

Next to him Samantha smothered a yawn. "How much farther?"

"A couple of hours." Leaning, Alex kissed her softly. "Go to sleep," he urged. "Tomorrow will be a long day."

Chapter Nine

The next morning, Samantha carried Gabe into the parlor of the three-room penthouse suite to find Gram and Mattie already up and eating breakfast.

This, Samantha decided as she added bacon to her plate, was going to be a day of indulgence. Starting with forbidden foods and ending with forbidden love.

"So." She dug into her breakfast. "I have a wedding dress to buy and only nine hours to do it. Anyone up for a shopping spree?"

Actually, she needed wedding everything: shoes, hose, veil, under things.

Gram patted her mouth with a napkin, then picked up a paper beside her plate. "Alex has provided us with an itinerary. After breakfast you have a meeting with the hotel wedding consultant. He has a note here not to worry about the cost. He wants the day to be special for you."

"Kiss up," Mattie muttered into her coffee.

"Matilda Ann," Gram protested mildly.

"Well, he is," Mattie said in defense.

Samantha simply grinned. "I hope so," she taunted, before biting off the end of a piece of bacon.

"Enough bickering, girls." Gram put her foot down. "We have too much to do today." She waved the itinerary. "After your meeting with the consultant, we go downtown to file for the marriage license. Then we shop for your gown and accessories. At two, the three of us have appointments at the hotel salon to have our hair and makeup done."

"Sounds like he's thought of everything," Mattie muttered.

"We're supposed to drop Gabe off with the men before our first appointment." Gram bustled to her feet. "We better get going, or we'll be running late all day. I'm going to grab my purse then I'm ready to go." She headed for the room she'd shared with Mattie.

"I need to get my purse, too." Mattie started to follow her grandmother.

"Mattie, wait." Samantha stopped her new friend. "I was wondering. Will you be my maid of honor?"

She waited with bated breath for Mattie's reaction. Though they'd connected from the very first moment, their friendship was still new.

Mattie didn't miss a beat. She stepped forward and wrapped her arms around Samantha and Gabe, squeezing hard. "I'd be honored." When she moved back, tears glistened in Mattie's eyes. "Now let's get going before we both start blubbering."

In her room, Samantha gathered her purse and Gabe's things.

She had an agenda of her own today. As soon as she'd accepted Alex's proposal, she'd made an appointment with her doctor to get started on birth control. The doctor warned her to let her system adjust to the pill before relying on it. He'd suggested using condoms for the first thirty days.

Which meant sometime today, Samantha needed to buy some condoms. Preferably without Gram looking over her shoulder.

Samantha stood staring at the bride waiting by the fountain. Elegant and poised in a fitted full-length dress in a soft creamy brocade that draped softly to the floor in a foot-long train, she held a bouquet of short-stemmed roses the same cream color as her dress. Nothing detracted from the line of the dress except the soft curves it covered: no ribbons, no lace, no beads. Sleeveless, the bride wore above-elbow-length gloves decorated with three elegant satin bows at the top of each.

She looked chic, sophisticated, beautiful.

Samantha could hardly believe she was the woman reflected in the mirror across the plaza. How could she look so calm when her knees were shaking. The dress made the difference, made her feel special.

She fingered her hair, wondering if she should have gone with a veil after all. She'd chosen to wear her hair up with a single fresh rose and a sprig of baby's breath as the only adornment. A few loose blond tendrils framed her face.

Convincing Gram and Mattie she needed a moment alone had been amazingly easy. She'd simply stated she wanted to take a short walk to settle her nerves. They'd agreed to meet here by the fountain at ten to four.

She clutched the small brown paper bag holding the condoms. She hadn't thought ahead to what she was going to do with her purchase during the wedding. The straight line of her dress didn't allow for any hiding places.

"Samantha Dell?" a deep male voice asked.

Samantha turned to find a tall dark-haired man dressed in a tux standing two feet away. "Yes."

"I'm Brock Sullivan. Gram told me I would find you here."

"Brock?" Shocked, she stared into the thin face dominated by sapphire-blue eyes. Sullivan blue eyes. Brock Sullivan, the long-lost brother. His military background evident in his stance and bearing. "Oh, my God. Does Alex know you're here?"

He nodded. "I got here about twenty minutes ago. Surprised the hell out of everyone."

"I'll bet you did." She held out her hand and squeezed his fingers when he offered his. "I'm pleased to meet you. I'm glad you're here for Alex."

A spark of humor lit his eyes but showed nowhere else on his face. "I had to come. Alex and I made a pact years ago to be each other's best man. That's why I sought you out. Alex wanted to be sure you'd be okay with me acting as his best man."

"Me?" she asked, surprised by his comment. "Why should I object?"

He hesitated before answering, assessing her seriously for a moment. "Because I was his best man at his first wedding. He didn't want you to be upset by a repeat performance."

Her heart twisted. How like Alex to be sensitive to her feelings. His thoughtfulness touched her deeply, and she meant it when she said, "It's up to Alex to choose who he wants to stand up for him. If you made a pact, then of course you have to be his best man."

"Thanks. You're a class act, Samantha."

"You came a long way to be here today. Where'd you fly in from? Somewhere in South America, wasn't it?"

"Something like that." He reached into the pocket of his black dress pants and pulled out a small jeweler's box. "Rett asked me to give you this."

Excited, she opened the box. "It's Alex's ring." She ran her finger over the platinum ring edged in gold, the center cut out in a Greek key pattern. "Beautiful. Thank you."

"Hey, I'm just the messenger. Rett's the genius."

"He certainly is." She raised pleading eyes to his. "But you can be my hero if you'll hold this bag until after the ceremony." Indicating her person, she said, "I don't have anywhere to carry it."

"Sure," he agreed easily, taking the bag and slipping it into his pants pocket. His tux jacket covered the slight bulge making it indiscernible. He held out his arm. "May I escort you to your wedding?"

"Thank you." She slipped her gloved hand through the crook of his elbow.

* * *

In the soft shadows of the garden, in a gazebo festooned in ivy and climbing roses, with family standing witness, Samantha exchanged her vows with Alex.

"I now pronounce you man and wife," the justice of the peace proclaimed in a loud voice for all to hear. "You may kiss the bride."

Samantha looked into Alex's blue eyes and with a rush of goose bumps it hit her. She was falling in love with him. His integrity, his thoughtfulness, his sense of duty, his love for family, even his stubbornness and pragmatism.

She held her breath, waiting for the feeling to fade and common sense to kick in. But when she became lightheaded from lack of air and the feeling remained, she released her breath in a soft whoosh of acceptance.

Oh, God. The realization thrilled her, scared her. Both for the same reason. She'd just married the man she loved. But he didn't love her. She felt sick to her stomach and euphoric at the same time. Looking into his eyes, seeing affection and desire, she decided to focus on the positive, on the joy, on the part of her dream coming true.

As long as she kept her emotions to herself, everything should be fine.

When his lips settled on hers in a warm kiss, she said a small prayer that everything would turn out all right for the three of them. Then she thought only of Alex as she returned his kiss in a silent pledge of commitment.

"Ladies and gentlemen, I present Mr. and Mrs. Alex Sullivan."

With the announcement, Samantha and Alex turned to accept good wishes and congratulations. She passed from one pair of arms to the next. Alex followed in her wake, receiving hardy pats on the back and hugs from all.

When the group broke apart, Alex laced his fingers with hers again. Touched by his nearness and support, Samantha savored this moment. His possessiveness and apparent devotion seemed so natural she almost believed it herself.

Soon Mattie shepherded them inside for the reception. Samantha carried Gabe, including him in the family unit. He grinned and held on tight.

As soon as they reached the penthouse suite and everyone had a glass of champagne, Gram approached Samantha. "My dear." Gram kissed Samantha's cheek. "Welcome to the family."

"Thank you." Samantha blushed with pleasure, pleased with the sentiment and the support Gram had given her these past few days, especially when Samantha knew Gram hadn't approved of the speed with which they'd married.

The enveloping sense of acceptance was like nothing Samantha had ever known. She'd loved her mother and her sister and had been loved in return, she knew, but it hadn't equaled what the Sullivans shared.

Sleepy, but too excited to be put down for a nap, Gabe began to fuss. Without breaking off his conversation with his brothers, Alex took the baby and settled him against his shoulder. Gabe immediately put his head down, and she knew he'd soon be asleep. While the men talked basketball, then sports in general, Samantha turned sideways to chat with Gram and Mattie.

Though they stood angled away from each other, nearly back-to-back, Alex kept his grip on Samantha's fingers. The link warmed her on an elemental level she barely recognized, but cherished nonetheless. After a few minutes, he moved his hand to the small of her back and suggested they start the buffet line.

The rest of the family followed. As they did for the rest of the evening. Watching Alex direct the activities, dinner, pictures, cake, Samantha noticed everyone followed his lead. It was subtle, more a deference than anything else, but a sure sign of respect that these self-reliant, even masterful, men accepted Alex as their natural leader.

No wonder he had such an awesome sense of responsibility. With such a large family relying on him, it would take a strong man with broad shoulders to carry the load.

She made a promise to herself to help him in any way she could. She refused to increase his burden by adding her weight to his shoulders.

Smiling at Ford's joke about a bartender and a talking duck, Samantha stifled a yawn.

"That's my cue," Alex whispered in her ear. "Don't give out on me now, the best part of the night is ahead of us."

She shook her head denying her fatigue. "I'm fine.

It's been a perfect day.'' She reached up to straighten his impeccable bow tie, looking up at him suggestively through her lashes. "But I'm ready to get out of these clothes and start our perfect night."

His gaze on her lips, he swallowed hard, then cleared his throat and announced, "Samantha and I would like to thank you all for joining us on this special day. We're going to make our escape. Everyone go out and have some fun. And have a safe trip home."

So saying, he passed a sleeping Gabe to Gram, and began to lead Samantha to the door. Family immediately swarmed around to wish them good-night.

Brock took advantage of the chaos to slip her the little brown bag. Grateful that he'd remembered, she kissed him on the cheek. "I'm so glad you were here today. I know it made a difference to Alex."

He inclined his head, his dark eyes sober. "It mattered to me, too."

Finally, Alex claimed her hand again, and they broke away from the crowd. "I had your things moved into my room earlier," he said as he opened the door to another suite.

"You think of everything." She ran her hand down the sleeve of his tux, enjoying the feel of muscle under the expensive fabric.

Samantha had an impression of subdued elegance, ivory and gold with an ancient Roman influence. The drapes were pulled back from the floor-to-ceiling window showcasing the spectacular view of the Las Vegas strip in all its nighttime glory.

With a sigh of relief she kicked off her shoes, dug

her toes into the lush cream carpeting and turned her back on the lavish display of lights to face her new husband.

Anticipation hummed through her blood.

Alex had shrugged out of his jacket and stood over an ice bucket on a pedestal table. "Looks like the hotel thought of the champagne," he said as he worked the cork free. He controlled the pop, poured the wine, handed her a glass and touched his softly against hers. "Alone at last."

She sipped, then stood on her toes to press her lips to his. "At last," she said against his mouth.

He deepened the kiss, thrusting his tongue in to slide over hers. She found the friction and taste of him more intoxicating than the wine. She leaned into him, her breasts flattening against his silk-clad chest. His arms circled her waist, pulled her closer. Warmth flowed through her, the physical heat of finally being in his arms and the emotional glow of the rightness of it.

Lifting her hands to his neck, she banged his head with the wineglass she still held. She laughed, flicking her gaze to his.

An answering gleam lit his blue eyes. He took her glass and the one he held and set them on the table. The brown paper bag caught his eye. "What's in the bag?"

"Condoms."

He lifted his brows. "I thought you told me your doctor started you on the pill."

"He did." Samantha folded her hands in front of her, a little anxious about the conversation. She so wanted everything to be perfect tonight. "But that was only a week ago. He advised using an alternative birth control for the first month while my body becomes regulated to the pill. I figured you'd want to take the necessary precautions."

"You figured right. So where does Brock fit into this? I saw him hand you the bag."

She smiled ruefully. "I wasn't about to buy condoms while I was with your grandmother, and she wasn't easy to dodge. I pleaded for a few minutes alone before the ceremony and sneaked off to the gift shop. Trouble was I had no pockets and no purse. Brock agreed to hold the bag for me."

Alex frowned. "Did he know what it was?"

"Not unless he peeked." She rubbed her hand down his chest, soothing him. "What's wrong? Brock's a big boy. I'm sure he realizes we're going to have sex tonight."

"You should have called me. I'd have taken care of it."

Yes, he would have. But she didn't need him to take care of her. She refused to be another burden to him. "I didn't think of it. Besides, I can handle buying condoms. I just had nowhere to put them."

"Next time call me. The thought of my brother, my wife and condoms is not an image I want to contemplate." He kissed her, stamping his possession on her with his mouth, claiming her body with bold demanding caresses. He stopped when she lay lax against him, her bones melted under the fiery assault.

"Come with me." Picking up the brown bag, he wrapped his arm around her waist.

In the bedroom, he tossed the bag on the night-stand. Then turned on the bedside light to reveal the blaze of passion in his gaze when he cupped her hand in his and kissed her palm, her forearm, the curve of her elbow. She shivered as his mouth continued up, ending in the arch of her shoulder and neck where he nibbled on the tender flesh of her throat.

"Alex." Her breath hitched on his name when his teeth sank into her earlobe. Desire drained her muscles of strength. "I can't stand much longer."

"You won't have to." Heat tickled her ear with his whispered words. He worked his hand under the fall of her hair to loosen the button on the keyhole closure at the top of her dress. "I can't wait to have you under me in bed."

"Hmm." She let her head fall forward, allowing him better access. In a slow spine-tingling caress, he lowered her zipper from between her shoulder blades to the small of her back. "I can't wait to have *you* under *me* in bed."

He laughed, a rough growl of delight. "Now, I won't be able to stand much longer."

Savoring the press of him against her stomach, she rubbed her hips back and forth. "Oh, I think you're standing up just fine."

"Darling, you haven't seen anything yet."

They had to buy a second box of condoms. And twice they'd been frantic for each other only to find the extra protection too far away, so they'd taken the chance the pills were doing the job.

Samantha rolled off Alex onto the floor next to

him. Her breasts heaved with the need for air. Sweat gleamed on her body. She felt limp as a rag doll. And utterly and entirely satisfied.

Next to her Alex's body glistened with the same dew as hers, his passion appeased for the moment.

There was no question they clicked on a physical level.

As her heart began to settle, Samantha laughed. "I can't believe we did that."

"Why not?" He rolled his head to look at her. "We've been doing that every other minute all weekend."

"I know, but the bellboy's going to be here soon to pick up the luggage. And our flight is in a couple of hours."

"And your point is?"

She laughed at his audacity. "My point is we didn't have time for this. If we don't get a move on, the bellboy will get quite an eyeful."

He rolled over, pinning her under his weight, devilment dancing in his eyes. "I'm willing if you are."

"Get off me." She pushed at his chest, her fingers automatically threading through the damp curls covering the hard muscles. The touch tempted her to ignore the feeling of gratification stealing her energy and go for a repeat performance, but they did have a plane to catch. "I'm grabbing a shower before the bellboy gets here."

He pushed up and off her, the impressive show of strength sent a tingling warmth through her. It took her a moment to realize he held his hand out to help her up.

"Thanks." She accepted his help, but once on her feet quickly turned away to gather her clothes rather than give in to temptation. "I'll be out in a moment."

He followed close behind her. "It'll go faster if we shower together."

She stopped, swung around. "Oh, no. Forget it. It'll take twice as long if we shower together."

He wrapped his hands around her waist, swept her along. "We'll be quick. I promise."

"Okay," she conceded as he assisted her into the shower stall. "But behave yourself."

Alex behaved extraordinarily well. His playfulness charmed and seduced her. He so rarely let loose of his sense of responsibility that she had no heart for squashing his uncharacteristic frivolity.

And why should she?

Flights left every hour for San Diego. And Cole who'd be picking them up from the airport was easy enough to reschedule. An hour or two delay wouldn't make a difference.

But it meant a world of difference to Alex. It meant a moment of freedom from the strict restraints he enforced on himself. Without doubt the extra hour of play was the most precious gift she could give him.

Running soap-slick fingers down his back, she rested her head on his shoulder.

Suddenly he stilled, lifted his head. "Someone's at the door."

"The bellboy," they said in unison.

Watching his eyes, she pulled his mouth down to hers and said against his lips, "He can come back later."

They missed their flight.

Chapter Ten

Alex carried Samantha over the threshold of his home. He didn't know why he made the romantic gesture when romance had no place in their relationship, but it seemed appropriate.

From the warm smile Samantha bestowed on him she appreciated the moment. Which was enough to make him feel good about it.

And he found that fact to be both worrisome and right.

A flash of memory brought back the moment when he last carried a woman into his home to start a life together. How different he'd felt then, than he did now. He'd been in love, yes. But what an illusion that had been.

He wouldn't make the same mistakes again. He was more mature, more confident, more in control this time. And the woman in his arms matched him in every way. Better than love her, he admired her and respected her. And a relationship based on mutual goals and companionship had a much better chance of success than one based on flimsy emotions.

And the amazing passion didn't hurt, either.

"Welcome home," he said, setting her down on the hardwood floor of the entry.

"We never did get around to gambling."

Alex met Samantha's gaze in a moment of silent communication. He'd kept her so busy in their room they hadn't gambled at all. At least not with money.

Only fair considering they'd both taken a bigger gamble with their lives. But so far so good. In fact, he hoped the rest of their marriage went as well as the last two days.

She smiled. "This is where it starts."

He shook his head. "No. It started last Friday, this is where the fun begins."

"Oh." She lifted her brows suggestively as she started forward. "I thought the last two days were plenty fun."

He suppressed a grin, following her into the living room. He did enjoy the way she made him laugh. "When you're right, you're right. Hi, Gram." He greeted his grandmother with a kiss on the cheek. "Thanks for watching Gabe."

Samantha went straight to Gabe who was asleep in his playpen.

"My pleasure." Gram fluttered her hand, the diamonds in her wedding set flashing as she waved off his gratitude. "I enjoyed having someone to fuss over for a change. The big place gets a little lonely these days."

"If you need anything, you only have to say so." Alex disliked the idea of Gram alone in the old family home. He'd suggested more than once she get a companion to stay with her.

"Away with you. I don't need a thing. I'm just saying I enjoyed the company." She sent him a stern look. "But don't start with your talk of having someone stay with me. I'm fine by myself. Cole didn't come in?"

"He had a date so he just dropped us off." Samantha also gave Gram a kiss before settling into the corner of the couch.

Alex took his turn checking on Gabe. He slept peacefully, his giraffe tucked under his head as a pillow. Alex reluctantly admitted he'd missed the little guy.

The peace of being home clicked into place.

"We're going to go get pizza in a little bit," Samantha said to Gram. "I hope you'll join us."

"Thank you, dear, but I don't want to impose on your first night together as a family."

Alex watched Samantha, waiting to see how she answered Gram. This moment would tell him how the future would go. As the oldest, he took his responsibility to his family very seriously. Best Samantha learn right from the start his family would always be welcome wherever he was.

"You are family," Samantha said easily, and Alex relaxed. "We're happy to have you with us." She turned to him. "After dinner, I should go over to my old place and pack up a few things."

"The movers already did all that," Gram assured her. "They moved all your things yesterday."

"Movers?" Samantha voiced her confusion.

"I forgot to tell you I hired a moving company to move your stuff over the weekend," Alex said.

"But I wasn't packed."

"They packed for you. The boxes are in the spare room. I had them put your furniture in storage."

"Storage?"

Maybe he should have discussed the disposition of her things with her before he hired the movers. He had just wanted to save her the time and effort by having the job done before they returned from Las Vegas.

"Don't worry, Samantha, Mattie and I oversaw the packing. Nothing was broken and it's all accounted for." Gram reassured Samantha. "And we made sure all the boxes were labeled with the contents."

"Thank you, Gram." Samantha reached over and squeezed Gram's hand in gratitude. She shot Alex a speaking glance. "I'd be devastated if I lost any family mementos."

"Of course, dear." Gram sympathized. "Don't mind Alex, he meant well. Men just don't understand women prefer to do some things themselves. That we take comfort in having some of our own things around us."

"Okay, enough," he protested. He'd only wanted to make Samantha happy. "If Samantha wants to move in some of her furniture, she's free to make any changes she wants."

* * *

Samantha pulled the brush through her hair in the bathroom off the master bedroom. She wore the barely there, white nightgown Mattie had given her. She'd been primping for a good ten minutes. Five minutes longer than necessary, but she felt a little strange about facing Alex.

Tonight was different than being with him in Las Vegas. That had been a time and place out of the ordinary. Their honeymoon, when they were both away from their normal surroundings and therefore on equal ground.

Tonight joining her new husband in his bed was the real start to their married life. She could hardly wait, yet the very thought scared her to death.

Two days spent in a sensual wonderland of erotic delight had made her realize she'd been fooling herself. There was no way she could keep her emotions separate from her physical response. She doubted she'd make it through the night without giving herself away.

So she wouldn't try.

Instead she'd keep the words to herself, but she'd live a life of love. She'd give freely to both Alex and Gabe and create the foundation for the family the three of them could truly be. And maybe, just maybe, Alex would learn to love her.

She set her brush on her mother's vanity mirror on the marble countertop. Gram and Mattie's thoughtfulness in placing some of Samantha's things out touched her. Alex's family had gone to a lot of trouble to make her feel welcome. Not one of them seemed to doubt the possibility of Alex loving her.

Hope bloomed within her and it felt good. It felt right. No more suppressing her feelings. Alex would just have to learn to live with her love. And somewhere along the line she'd teach him to love Gabe, too.

"Samantha?" A knock sounded at the door and Alex asked, "Are you okay?"

She opened the door, struck a seductive pose. "I'm not just okay. I'm really, really good."

Alex's gaze swept from her carefully tousled hair to her pink-tipped toes. The look in his eyes had changed from weary to passionate by the time they returned to hers. He reached for her, pulled her against him and lowered his mouth to hers.

Rising into his embrace, she ringed her arms around his neck welcoming the feel of him against her.

"Honey—" he bore her back onto the bed "—you're better than good, you're bad."

In the weeks following their wedding, life fell into a pleasant routine. Marrying her was the smartest thing Alex had ever done. With Samantha moved in Gabe settled right down, quickly gaining back the weight he'd lost while alone with Alex.

The baby's decline had really worried Alex. If Samantha had continued to refuse his proposal, he probably would have moved in with Gram until Gabe adjusted to his new situation. It would have been inconvenient, but Alex had learned firsthand how fragile babies were; he'd do anything—anything—to keep from losing another child.

His daughter had been a part of his life for such a short time. He'd slowly accustomed himself to the thought of having a child, but the first time he'd felt the flutter of her movement in the womb, he'd fallen hard and fast. He'd had his heart torn out once; he couldn't live through that pain again.

Luckily, Samantha had changed her mind. And life was good. Really good.

Samantha dropped Gabe off at the day care in the morning and Alex picked him up in the evenings, except on nights when he had a meeting scheduled, like tonight's parent, teacher, student association meeting set for six o'clock.

He could have run home for a quick bite to eat with Samantha and Gabe, but he preferred to stay and work. He had plenty to do, and he found it easier to get home late than to tear himself away. And he liked when Samantha waited to eat with him.

He liked lots of things about her, that she made him laugh, that she made him think, that she made him a better man. Best of all he liked that bitter memories and past hurts seemed to matter less when he was with her.

The schedule they'd worked out over the past few weeks allowed him an hour or so of quality time with his son most evenings. Alex usually went through the mail while Gabe played in his playpen.

Alex knew he should make better use of the time, but his gut clenched whenever he thought about getting closer to the kid.

He'd do anything for him, anything but love him.

Anything but trust his heart to this vulnerable, de-

pendent, fragile little being. He tried. Alex knew his
fear wasn't rational, knew he was in denial, but for
once, self-preservation exceeded his monumental control.

Which was probably why his son still called him
"man."

A knock sounded at his open door.

"Hello, handsome." Samantha walked in carrying
Gabe in one arm and a white bag with golden arches
in the other. The salt and oil scent of French fries
flooded the room.

"Hello, beautiful." Alex rose to round the desk.
Dressed in her smock, pale blue with yellow happy
faces, and white pants she looked as fresh now as
when he'd left the house this morning. Her hair fell
in a soft slide past her shoulders. A pink blush of
pleasure added color to her cheeks, and she licked her
lips, bringing a sheen to her pretty mouth.

He experienced an undeniable desire to muss her
up. "What are you doing here?"

"I know you missed lunch, so I thought you'd be
hungry. I brought dinner."

"Perfect timing. I'm starved."

Taking the bag he set it on the desk then reached
for her. He pulled her to him for a long hot kiss.
Tangling his fingers in the golden ribbons of her hair,
he tilted her head to deepen the kiss.

Feeling a tug at his hair, he smiled against her
mouth. Gabe did not appreciate being ignored. After
one last quick kiss, Alex lifted his head, reaching up
as he did so to loosen Gabe's grip on his hair.

Alex put his nose right up against Gabe's. "Hey, big guy, let go."

Gabe's eyes opened wide. He giggled then reached up to grab two fistfuls of hair.

Wincing, Alex took him from Samantha, tickling his fingers into Gabe's ribs until the boy released his hold. Freed, Alex set Gabe on his feet.

He immediately held his arms up demanding, "Man, up."

Alex hiked him up again, playing tickle games while Samantha unpacked the food. When she had everything ready, Alex plopped Gabe on his butt on the floor and distracted him with a soccer ball that had somehow found its way into his office.

Then, grabbing two waters from the minifridge in the corner, Alex joined her in the guest chairs facing his desk, sprawling so his knee bumped hers. Leaning back, he sighed in satisfaction.

"The food looks great, too," he told her. "But you didn't have to go out of your way."

"It was no trouble. Gabe and I miss you when you have to work late. He'll sleep better now that he's seen you."

He lifted an eyebrow, watching her as he munched a fry. "You're making that up."

"I'm not," she insisted, a half smile lifting the corner of her mouth. "He's a little terror on the nights you're away."

"Hard to believe a month ago I couldn't get the kid to sleep without a drive in the car."

"Which proves my point. Kids are creatures of habit. They react to a change in routine."

"So it's not me he misses at all. Any 'man' would do." Though he shouldn't care, the words left a bad taste in his mouth.

Her green eyes admonished him over a bite of burger. "That's not what I mean at all. And you know it." She rubbed her hand over Gabe's dark curls as he used her leg to steady himself.

He opened and closed his fist in a sign he wanted a bite. Samantha handed him a fry. He stuffed the whole thing in his mouth and worked his fist again.

She shook her finger at him. "Chew first, then you can have another."

Not liking that answer, Gabe sidestepped from her to Alex and made his gimme motion. Alex handed him a fry.

"Hey!" Samantha protested.

Alex shrugged. "We guys have to stick together."

"He'll choke."

"He's fine."

"Alex," she gasped, excitement lighting her eyes, "he's walking!"

Alex looked down to see Gabe take a step. "My God." Quick as a flash, Alex stuck out a hand ready to catch Gabe when he started to teeter.

Gabe grabbed on long enough to steady himself then took off again toward the soccer ball. When he reached for the ball, he wobbled and fell on his butt. Surprised, his little face started to crumple until Samantha began to clap.

Delighted by his prowess, she jumped to her feet and swept Gabe into her arms for a celebratory hug.

"You wonderful boy, you walked. Did you see, Alex? He walked."

"He sure did." Inexplicable pride brought Alex to his feet. He joined Samantha, rubbing Gabe on the head. "Good going, kid. Put him down, let's see if he'll walk to you."

"Okay." She kissed Gabe and set him on his feet. Alex held him while she backed a few feet away then held out her arms. "Come on, Gabe, come to Mama."

"Mama." Confused by the sudden attention, Gabe looked from Samantha to Alex and back again. She beckoned to him with both hands. Grinning, Gabe began to walk toward her, but he kept hold of Alex's finger.

Smiling, she encouraged and praised him all the while scooting back creating more space between them so he had to let go of Alex to reach her. He did, taking three steps on his own before tumbling into her arms. After hugs and kisses, she immediately turned him around to send him back to Alex.

"Go to Daddy, Gabe. Go to Daddy."

"Come on, kid," Alex urged, "show me how you can walk."

Thrilled with his new talent, Gabe giggled and rushed across the carpet to Alex. He couldn't describe his feelings seeing the joy on his son's face, knowing he trusted Alex to keep him from falling, to keep him safe.

Alex's gaze met Samantha's in an instant of shared exaltation. He'd never known a moment such as this, never remembered a moment of such simple enjoyment, and it pleased him to share it with Samantha.

Her green eyes gleamed. "You know there's no going back now he's found his feet."

Alex shrugged, feigning indifference. Truthfully, he couldn't help but look forward to the chase ahead.

The game continued until the phone rang, calling Alex to duty. Chagrined, he realized he'd forgotten his meeting. He couldn't remember the last time he'd forgotten an appointment.

"Sorry, I've got to go." He finished his last bite of burger, sipped the last swig of water and tossed the empties in the trash. Then stopped to give Samantha a lingering kiss before he chucked Gabe under the chin and headed out the door.

"Alex," she called, delaying his departure.

He turned back to find himself caught in her earnest gaze.

"You aren't an interchangeable being in Gabe's life, you're his father. And he might call you something besides 'man,' if you called him something other than 'kid.'"

He frowned but nodded. "I'll try harder."

Samantha used her lunch break to drive into San Diego. She had a special purchase to make: a home pregnancy test. Tests. She could have no doubt of the results before she faced Alex with the news. And though having a child of her own would fulfill her heart's desire, she seriously hoped the tests turned out negative.

The timing just stank.

Her hands shook on the wheel with excitement, with anxiety. Because she understood the last thing

Alex needed right now was another child added to the equation. Yet she loved him and nothing would make her happier than to be pregnant with their child.

All the reasons she'd agreed to marry him still existed. The past month had proved that father and son needed her. Yes, they'd grown closer, but they still had a long way to go before trust evolved and love developed between them.

Adding another baby to the mix risked jeopardizing the fragile bond building between Alex and Gabe.

Bypassing Alpine, she pulled into the Wal-Mart parking lot in El Cajon. She was taking no chance of running into someone who knew her or Alex. If it turned out she was pregnant, she wanted to be the one to give him the news. Not a local gossipmonger.

Two hours and three tests later, she stared at the three different test sticks.

Her heart beat a wild tattoo of triumph mixed with dismay.

The results were all the same.

Positive. Positive. Positive.

All she needed was the doctor's confirmation to make it unanimous. She'd already called for an appointment. It was set for Thursday at nine. But she knew, every female instinct she possessed told her she carried a child. Alex's child. She felt blessed. And cursed. Joy. And despair.

And more than a little guilty. Because she wanted this baby so much, and she knew Alex didn't.

She honestly didn't know how she'd live with the secret until the doctor made the confirmation. Somehow she'd manage. Despite her intuition, she didn't dare jump the gun on this announcement.

No way could she drop this kind of bombshell on Alex, only to say, "never mind," two days later. He had a great sense of humor, but it didn't stretch that far.

Carefully, she brown-bagged the evidence and carried the bag out to the trash in the yard. She didn't want Alex stumbling over the test results before she had a chance to tell him the good news.

Samantha's trip into San Diego threw off her schedule. She got home late to find Alex had started cooking dinner. While he finished the meal, she fed Gabe and settled him down for the night.

She came up behind Alex at the sink, wrapped her arms around his waist and nipped his ear. He smelled better than the chicken baking in the oven. "Gabe's waiting for you. Why don't you go say good-night, and I'll set the table."

He turned, caught her to him and lowered his head to steal a kiss. He took his time savoring her mouth before raising his head. "Emily said he literally ran her ragged today."

Samantha grinned and nodded. "He's pretty worn-out. You better hurry or you'll miss him."

He handed her the oven mitts. "The chicken only needs a couple of minutes more. Pour the wine, I'll be right back."

Samantha opened the cupboard, took down two glasses, wine for Alex, water for her. No wine for her tonight, or any other night for the next eight months.

A pang of regret for the loss of the companionable time spent over a relaxing glass of wine in the evenings hit her. An unreasonable reaction since it wasn't the wine that made the occasions special but the time spent together. That wouldn't change.

At least she hoped not.

Still, it was the first of many differences to come. She looked forward to each and every one. She was so tempted to tell Alex, wanting to share each new discovery with him. She fought back the impulse, knowing her instinct to have the doctor's confirmation was a sound decision.

Alex returned just as she finished setting the table. He smiled wryly, taking his seat. "You were right. I tucked him in, but he was already out. With luck he'll sleep through the night."

She toasted him with her mug. "Amen to that." For all the improvement he'd made, Gabe still suffered from an occasional nightmare. She dug into the baked chicken. "Hmm. This is good," she complimented him. "I should let you cook more often."

He shrugged. "I don't mind cooking, but I don't get into anything too complicated."

They went on to discuss the events of the day and their plans for the rest of the week. When silence fell, it was a comfortable quietness. These moments of simple contentment along with the times of heated passion encouraged Samantha to believe her love might someday be returned.

She prayed the baby she carried would link them as a true family.

Sighing, she placed her fork on her empty plate and sat back in her chair. "Wonderful. Thanks."

Alex leaned forward to refill her water. The look he sent her held a sensual promise. "I know just how you can show your gratitude."

She rolled her eyes at him before beginning to gather the dirty dishes. "Don't get any ideas until the kitchen is clean."

"Spoilsport." He took the plates from her and carried them to the dishwasher.

Samantha admired his efficient movements as he dealt with the chore. His graceful economy of motion started her thinking of other ways he was good at using his body. She did have one question though. "Aren't you going to rinse those dishes?"

He looked at her in surprise. "Why would I rinse them when they're going in the dishwasher?"

Typical male thinking. "Because the food sticks to the plates?"

"Sometimes. I just leave it in for the next load, that usually takes care of it."

"I see." A smile tugged at the corner of her mouth. Oh, yeah, typical. But the revelation reassured her somehow, made him seem a little less intimidating. A little less in control of everything.

She gently nudged him aside. "I'll finish in here while you take out the trash."

Dishes being one of Alex's least favorite things to do, he readily agreed. Unfortunately, the plastic bag gave out right as he reached the trash can. Stifling a curse, he gathered what he could into the wrecked bag and lifted the lid to the trash can. Spying a brown paper bag on top, he emptied the contents, intending to use the bag to hold the spilled trash on the ground.

All coherent thought left his head when three cardboard boxes fell into view.

Home pregnancy tests.

"Damn it." His stomach began to churn as a vise closed around his heart. For a minute he did nothing but stare, refusing to contemplate what the evidence meant.

The damning evidence.

"Damn." His mood deteriorated along with his language. How could Samantha do this to him?

Stuffing a box in his back pocket, he cleaned up the trash mess and returned to the house.

She finished wiping down the counters when he entered the kitchen. She folded the tea towel, smiled at him.

He tossed the box in front of her.

"You want to tell me about this?" he demanded.

His hope that it was a misunderstanding disappeared along with the color from her face. She swayed and grabbed the counter to ground herself.

As fast as the blood left her head, it rushed to his. Rage consumed him. His hands shook. All the more furious for the shattered hope. He'd done it again, left himself open to betrayal. And he felt it like a fist to the gut.

Hooking her by the elbow, he guided her to the table. Pulling out a chair, he stuffed her into it.

"Alex," her voice entreated. She reached for his hand.

Stepping back, he crossed his arms over his chest. "Explain."

Her hands dropped to her lap and folded together, the knuckles showing white. "I knew you'd be upset."

"I'm way past upset. When did you plan on telling me?"

"Not until I had a doctor's confirmation." Guilt dimmed the green of her eyes, confirming his worst fears. "I wanted to be absolutely certain."

"You're certain now. There were three tests in the trash. What's the result, Samantha?" He made no effort to control the bite in his voice.

Samantha swallowed hard, forcing saliva down her dry throat. No, he wasn't taking this well at all. And it was about to get worse. "I'm pregnant."

His head snapped back as if he'd taken one on the chin. "Why doesn't that surprise me? How could you use me like this?"

She drew in a deep breath before answering. One of them needed to stay calm. "I didn't do anything alone, Alex. It took two to make this baby. You were right there with me when we took chances on our honeymoon."

"Don't tell me you want me to believe it was an accident." His laugh held no mirth. "How many times am I supposed to buy that story?"

"It isn't like that—"

"Isn't it?" He cut her off. "A woman who desperately wants a baby suddenly turns up pregnant with my child. Even though she knows I want no part of having kids. It seems just like that to me."

A terrible gnawing feeling spread under her heart, the feeling of something going horribly wrong while she was powerless to stop it.

Her blood grew ice cold, and her calm began to crack. "Okay, you can stop comparing me to your ex-wife and my sister now. I would never trick you the way they did."

"Right." The corner of his mouth lifted in a sneer, matched by the disdain in his eyes. "Because you're so up-front and honest. That's why it took you four months to tell me about my son. You probably had something like this planned all along."

"You don't believe that." She rubbed her hands over her arms to warm herself inside and out. She'd known he wouldn't be happy to hear she was pregnant. It never occurred to her that he would accuse her of deliberately tricking him. "I told you of the need to use condoms. We both knew the chance we were taking when we made love without them."

"I don't know what to believe," he raved. "I only have your word you were taking birth control at all. My God, I should just have sperm donor tattooed on my forehead."

He laughed harshly. "You know what makes it worse, what makes this so pathetic? I actually trusted you. More fool me."

He tossed her a look of disgust and disillusionment, then turned to leave. "I can't stand to even look at you."

Oh, no, Samantha had had enough. She jumped up, unintentionally digging her nails into his arm to swing him around. He'd had his say, now she'd have hers.

"I'm getting a little tired of your poor, poor pitiful me attitude." No one dismissed her child with disgust and got away with it.

She jabbed him in the chest with a stiff finger.

"So you had a crummy childhood. News flash, you're not the only one. At least you had your grandmother to help you. And the closeness you have with your brothers might not have existed except for the hardships you shared." No one called her a liar and got away with it.

Jab.

"Maybe you did deserve a few years of selfishness, of thinking of yourself first, but that time has past. You're only hanging on to it out of sheer stubbornness because you feel used. Well, I'm not the one who did that to you, and I won't be the one punished for it." No one questioned her honor and got away with it.

Jab.

"So get over it already." No one ripped out her heart and stomped on it.....

She bit her lip, swallowed hurt and disappointment along with the lump in her throat. She wanted to laugh as he had, but she feared it would be more a moan than a challenge. She lifted her chin, met him glare for glare, too angry to care if he saw her tears. She'd done nothing to betray him, but his distrust tore her heart from her chest.

"You want to hear pathetic?" she demanded. "Somewhere between when the judge gave you custody of Gabe and the honeymoon where our baby was conceived, I fell in love with you. I would no more do anything to hurt you than I would Gabe.'' She pushed past him intent on leaving the room, on leaving him. She didn't look back when she demanded, ''You tell me, who's the bigger fool?''

Chapter Eleven

Samantha packed up her things and Gabe's, belted him into his car seat and drove across town.

Gram took one look at the tears on Samantha's cheeks, at Gabe in her arms, at the suitcase on the porch and swung the door wide.

"I've left Alex," Samantha confessed.

"Come in, child. We'll get Gabe settled then have some tea and talk."

Gram's unflinching support touched Samantha as much as Alex's accusations and distrust devastated her.

The next few days passed in a haze of numb denial, of living minute to minute. She'd given Gram all the details of her argument with Alex, figuring it only fair considering Samantha had put Gram in the middle by seeking refuge in her home.

Not that Alex had made any attempt to contact Samantha.

Not that she cared, not that she'd talk to him if he did. She'd compromised her dreams once, only to have them thrown in her face. She deserved better, like being loved for herself, like having the father of her child cherish the thought of their baby, like having the home and the family and the dog she'd always wanted.

Other women had those things. She vowed she would, too. No more compromising.

Gram had been great, supportive without being judgmental. Samantha knew she'd spoken to Alex. Heard his side of events, but she hadn't tried to sway Samantha one way or another.

She'd planted herself firmly in the neutral zone.

She even attempted to persuade Samantha to stay for Sunday dinner. "I wish you would reconsider. You're family, too."

Right, that's why neither she nor Gabe had heard from Alex in three days. His silence spoke louder than words.

"Thanks, Gram, but I wouldn't feel comfortable. Are you sure you don't mind me leaving Gabe?"

"Gabe is always welcome, dear."

"Do me a favor, Gram. Make sure Gabe sits next to Alex. Don't let him distance himself by pawning Gabe off on you or Mattie."

Samantha would be damned if she'd let Alex get away with ignoring Gabe. She'd come too far to bring father and son together to give up now.

Besides, Alex had already fallen for Gabe, the little charmer. She'd seen the pride and affection Alex displayed when he forgot he wasn't supposed to care. He only had to make the realization himself.

Unfortunately, his stubbornness was only out-weighed by his pride.

Gram sent Samantha an approving nod. "I'm glad to see you haven't given up on him yet. I've always felt to blame for his attitude toward parenthood. He was such a help to me after his parents died. Even at fourteen he was so strong and capable, I think I relied on him more than I should have. He shouldered the responsibility without question. But I'm afraid it's left him a mite shortsighted when it comes to the joys of parenting."

Commiserating, yet despairing of Alex ever changing, Samantha met Gram's gaze over the set table. "I don't know how much more patient I can be, Gram. He's not just shortsighted regarding parenting. When it comes to all matters of the heart, he's blind as a bat."

Gram stopped peeling potatoes to face Samantha. "There's none so blind as those who refuse to see."

"What's that mean?"

"It means it takes two to work at a relationship. Alex has his faults. I'll not deny that. But child, I'm not sure anyone could live up to your ideal."

Samantha frowned. Gram must be confused. Samantha wasn't the one with impossible expectations.

"I understand he feels misused. Well, it wasn't by me. He has to understand I won't be punished for what others have done. I have my pride, too."

"I'm not talking about pride." Gram pulled Samantha down to sit beside her at the table. "I've listened to you talk these last few days about your mother and father and the dream you've always had to recapture a love like theirs."

"Yes," Samantha agreed a tad defensively. "Those were the happiest times of my life." Except for the last month with Alex and Gabe, but that was over now.

"Samantha, you have to remember your memories are those of a child." Gentle yet resolute, Gram made her point. "You don't truly know what the relationship was between your parents."

"I know my mother never found anyone to replace my father." The petulance in her voice appalled Samantha, making her sound like the child Gram referred to, but she couldn't help it. She felt threatened on a very elemental level.

"So you said," Gram agreed. "And I'm sad for her. But I have to wonder if it's because she gave herself a chance, or if she clung to a memory no man had a hope of matching."

Alex dribbled down the court, feinted right, dodged left and slam-dunked the ball.

"Yeah," he crowed, breathing hard. The exertion had worked off some of his tension. "Twenty-two to sixteen. I win. Want to play again?"

Doug waved him off. "Not a chance. Don't you have dinner at Gram's tonight?"

"I've got time." Alex used the tail of his T-shirt to wipe the sweat from his forehead.

Doug checked his watch. "I don't think Gram would agree."

"Nothing I do tonight will make Gram happy. She's on Samantha's side."

Doug stopped tying his shoe to eye Alex over the top of his sunglasses. "You haven't made up with Samantha yet? I confirmed two days ago she told the truth about the need for extra protection. You didn't use the extra protection, and you got caught. You can't blame her for the risk you both took."

"Can't I?" Alex demanded. "I have only her word she was even taking birth control pills."

"Are you even hearing yourself? Why would she lie about that, then tell you about the need for condoms? Lot easier to get pregnant without them."

Alex tossed the ball into his gear bag with more force than necessary. "I'm tired of being used as a sperm donor."

"Bull."

"What?"

"It's called accountability." Doug wiped a towel over his head and neck, then pulled his street shoes from his bag. "You've had enough psych classes getting your double master's to know you made the decision to have a child when you elected not to use protection on your honeymoon."

"You're giving me psychobabble?" Alex stared at his friend in disbelief.

"You like that?" Doug grinned heartlessly. "Here's more for you. Your denial is a manifestation of your fear of commitment. Samantha scares you so you've found a way to push her away."

"You don't know what you're talking about,"

Alex denied, but the disclaimer sounded hollow even to his ears.

"I know you've been happier in the last few months than I've seen you in years. She's the best thing that's ever happened to you, and you'd be a fool to let her get away."

Alex pulled into the drive at Gram's. The Estate, as they called the Victorian home surrounded by two acres of grounds, had a long drive that led to the garage and carport. His cousin, Mattie, lived in a converted apartment above the garage. He stopped between her Toyota and Cole's truck.

No sign of Samantha's car.

Probably parked in the garage to throw him off guard, then she'd be inside cooking or tidying, looking all homey. Hoping he'd see what he was missing.

He knew she'd run here after bundling up Gabe and rushing from the house. Gram had called him the next morning to demand what he'd done to chase away the best thing that ever happened to him.

"The best thing to ever happen to me," he'd responded, the words bitter on his tongue. "That's what you said when I married my ex."

"No," she calmly corrected him. "I never said that about your ex, she was too selfish, less giving. I always knew you could do better. And you have. If you're smart, you won't blow it."

"You need to go back to your source. I'm not the one to blame here."

"See, that's part of the problem, dear. The way I understand it, there's no blame to be placed."

Right, as if being used as a baby maker—again—could be forgiven.

The best thing to ever happen to him, bah. He climbed from his car. Didn't his friends and family understand she'd betrayed him?

Then again, he still had trouble reconciling Samantha's behavior. She'd fought so hard for everything she believed in, he'd felt sure she'd honor his request not to have more children. But no, she'd played him for a sucker from the very beginning.

Forget her little homemaker games. The only reason he was here was for Gram.

He entered the kitchen through the back door. The savory scent of roasting beef, steaming vegetables and baking apples hit him all at once. The sound of chatter and laughter told him he was home.

"Hey, Alex." His twin brothers hailed him even as Mattie sent him a chiding glare on her way out of the room.

No sign of Samantha in the kitchen.

Not that he was looking for her.

He made his way to the stove where Gram worked over the gravy. He hugged her without disturbing her flow. "Gram, how are you tonight? These boys helping you like they should?"

"Don't fuss." She sent him a look from the corners of her eyes. "Samantha helped me get things ready before she left."

"Samantha's not here?" Surprised, he glanced around, half expecting Samantha to appear and prove Gram wrong.

"No. She didn't want to intrude."

He frowned. "Where'd she go?"

"I can't say."

"Can't or won't."

Her wise blue eyes flashed dangerously when she turned on him. "Can't. She didn't offer the information, and I didn't ask. I just know she felt uncomfortable staying. Which didn't sit well with me, I can tell you." With a sniff she turned back to the stove. "Gabe's in the living room if you're interested."

Recognizing a dismissal when he heard one, he made his escape.

In the living room, Ford and Cole watched football. Mattie sprawled on the couch keeping an eye on Gabe, who sat on the floor playing with blocks.

He looked up when Alex came into the room. Gabe's face lit up. He popped up and ran in his wobbly gait to wrap himself around Alex's leg.

"Daddy!" He shouted gleefully and lifted his arms in a demand to be held.

"Gabe." Alex hefted his son into his arms. Hearing his son call him Daddy for the first time touched a chord deep inside him. Gabe cuddled against him, and his head settled on Alex's shoulder. His heart expanded to fill his whole chest.

In a heartbeat he fell in love.

Wanting to share the moment, he automatically glanced around, searching for Samantha before he remembered she wasn't there.

Disappointment deflated his elation. She should be here. With him. With Gabe. They were a family.

He'd been such a fool, an arrogant unfeeling fool, too worried about the forest to see the trees.

Cupping his son's head, he stepped out on the porch needing to be alone while he faced some truths.

Talk about being a fool. When he thought of the hateful things he'd said, he wondered why she hadn't taken Gabe and left the state. What courage it took her to leave her home behind to bring him his son. He'd never thanked her.

Instead he'd taken away her only family, coerced her into a loveless marriage and stolen her dream.

Then he insulted her by accusing her of lying, cheating and betrayal.

Meanwhile, she told him she loved him.

And he let her walk away.

He had to get her back. Tonight.

Instead of trusting in the contentment and joy of his new life, fear of being hurt again caused him to overreact when something innocent happened. Angry, bitter and distrustful, he'd let the past overwhelm his perspective of the present, of the future.

These last three days he'd been miserable. Miserable with missing her. And Gabe.

The two of them filled his life. They brought love and laughter and intelligent conversation into a home he'd let grow empty of happiness. Samantha was right, he shamed his family with his pursuit of a barren existence.

May Gram forgive him. And Samantha, too. He needed her, now more than ever. Not just as a mother for Gabe, or the child she carried, but as his wife and the best thing to ever happen to him.

Cuddling a sleeping Gabe close, Alex went inside. He had some apologizing to do. He found Gram fussing with the flowers on the dining-room table. Wrapping an arm around her shoulders he gave her a squeeze. "Thank you, Gram. Have I told you lately I love you."

She patted his hand with loving patience, glancing at him from the corners of her eyes. "I'm not the one you need to be telling."

He winked. "You're right, as usual. Tonight I plan to fix that."

Using the key Gram gave her, Samantha let herself into the quiet darkened house. She was later than she'd intended when she left for dinner and a movie. But she'd been so mad at herself for crying all through the movie, she'd stayed for the next showing.

She made her way to the room she shared with Gabe. The moment she walked in, she knew something was wrong. Gabe was gone.

Alex's voice came from the chair in the corner. "I had Cole take Gabe home. He's staying with him until we get there."

Samantha flipped on the lights and tossed her purse on the bed. She had the horrible feeling of having lived through this before. Hands on hips, she faced Alex.

"You took him from me again?" Unbelievable exhaustion and an unbearable sense of loss swamped her.

He stood and came to her, stopping short of touching her. "I haven't taken him from you. I want you to come home with me. With us."

Yeah, she'd definitely lived through this before.

And she didn't like where it had led. She wouldn't put herself through the pain of believing him again.

"No."

"I'm sorry. I know I hurt you."

She crossed her arms over her chest, to protect her heart, to keep him at a distance. "Exactly what are you sorry for?"

He stuffed his hands in his pockets, shuffled his feet. "For anything you want me to be sorry for."

Disappointment at his nonanswer bit deep. "So you're not really sorry for anything?"

"No. No." He sounded desperate. But desperate for what? "I'm sorry for everything. Sorry for accusing you of using me. Sorry for calling you a liar. Sorry for not trusting you."

With a great effort, Samantha held herself together. His apology sounded too good to be true, which meant it probably was.

"Why are you sorry?"

He ran a hand through his hair. In frustration or exasperation? Or nervousness? "Because I was wrong. You were right. Family rates above all else, and I've been selfish in closing myself off from Gabe, but we're past that now. He called me Daddy tonight." His eyes lit up and he reached for her. Cradling her cheeks in his palms, he leaned over her folded arms to kiss her.

She felt his joy, his excitement, his pride in his son. Tears flooded her eyes. She lowered the barrier of her arms and returned his kiss, sharing in his newfound love for Gabe. She'd hoped he'd eventually come around, but after the past few days she'd begun to doubt.

She was truly happy father and son had found each other.

It freed her to find her own future.

Alex ended the kiss and rested his forehead against hers. "How long will it take you to pack?"

She stepped back. "I'm happy for you and Gabe, but I'm not going with you."

All emotion drained from his expression. "Why not? I apologized."

"Yes, but not because you believe me. Not because you believe *in* me."

"Samantha, you're pregnant with my child. Gabe needs you. Being a family is everything you've always wanted."

"Not everything. Not love."

His eyebrows pulled together in a frown. Regret touched his eyes. "We have love, you said so. We both love Gabe and our child." He closed the distance between them, cupped her elbows, running his thumbs over the sensitive inner skin. "I care about you, Samantha. I respect you. You'll never want for anything, and I'll always be faithful. Isn't that enough?"

His touch awakened her senses just as his earnestness caused her throat to tighten and tears to well behind her eyes. He offered everything he could. And she wanted, oh how she wanted, to reach out and grab it.

But she wouldn't, she couldn't. Not this time.

If she compromised again, she'd regret it for the rest of her life.

Slowly, carefully, her heart breaking, she pulled away from his touch and walked to the door, holding it open.

"I'm sorry, Alex. I deserve to be loved for myself."

Alex slammed into his house after watching Cole drive away. Hands fisted at his side, he made for his weight room.

To work off his rage.

How could Samantha be so selfish? How could she put her needs before their children's needs? How could she not see they should be together?

He left the door ajar to listen for Gabe, sleeping down the hall.

Stripping off shirt, shoes, socks, he attacked the punching bag hanging from the beam ceiling. Bare knuckles connected with leather. Then again. Again. Each a satisfying thwack.

She'd led him on. Lured him in. Then turned him inside out and left him stranded. After he'd confessed his feelings for her.

So much for her declaration of love.

Sweat ran down his temples, his chest, his arms. Still he pounded.

Couldn't she see she was throwing away their future? And why? For some nebulous emotion she might never find. He'd opened his soul to her, offered her a giving, caring, passionate relationship, but was that enough? No.

She rejected him without regard to his feelings.

Stubborn unfeeling witch. He punctuated his frustration with a punch.

Selfish. Bam.

Manipulative. Bam.

Self-seeking. Bam.

Romantic. Bam.

Fool. Bam. Bam.

She loved him, and she was throwing it away.

A cry carried down the hall from Gabe's room. Alex grabbed the bag to stop it. He used his shirt to wipe the sweat from his forehead and the blood from his knuckles.

He found Gabe standing in his crib, tears welling from big blue eyes. He stopped crying when he saw Alex and waved his arms to be picked up.

"Hey, big boy. What's got you up?" Alex lifted Gabe and got his first clue. He plunked the baby down on the changing table and removed his dirty diaper.

Gabe looked up at him. "Mama?"

"Mama's not coming, son. She doesn't want to be with you and me." As the words left Alex's mouth, he realized they didn't sound right. Didn't feel right.

Samantha loved Gabe. She loved Alex. She wanted nothing more than to be there with them.

He was the reason she wasn't. Because he hadn't had the guts to ante up his feelings. Not only was she the best thing to ever happen to him, he loved her.

More, he needed her.

How many times this last week had he looked up to share a joke, an opinion, a quiet moment? How many times had he pounded his pillow to chase away the picture of her sloe-eyed with satisfaction? How many times had he turned on the TV to drown out the silence left by his absent family?

He'd missed her so much. But he'd been too self-absorbed to accept any of the responsibility for their breakup.

Alex stood over Gabe, cursing himself for his ineptitude. He'd blown it, and he'd blown it big.

How had he let things go so wrong?

She'd told him the truth about the baby. It only made sense. Why tell him about the need for condoms at all if her plan was to get pregnant on their honeymoon? As Doug had pointed out, her chances of success would have been a lot better if she'd kept the news to herself.

"Your mom possesses more integrity, more honesty, more generosity than any other woman I've known. I'll do anything to win her back."

"Daddy? Mama!" Two words that spoke volumes. Gabe wanted his mother and he expected his dad to bring her to him.

"I'm going to do my best, son. Come on. You stink and I'm sweaty." Lifting his son against his bare chest, Alex headed to the shower. "Tomorrow we go after your mom."

Tuesday evening Samantha arrived at Alex's to baby-sit while he attended a school-board meeting. She felt strange knocking on Alex's door. This was her home, not some place she had to ask permission to enter.

Maybe she'd been too rash in letting it go.

During the darkest loneliest part of the night, she'd replayed Gram's warning against setting impossible expectations. Samantha cherished her memories of her father, but she'd barely been six when he died. Perhaps basing her impressions of the ideal family on the perceptions of a six year old wasn't the smartest course of action.

She'd always thought of her mother's inability to find happiness in her relationships as a tribute to her love for Samantha's father. Now she realized that by creating impossible standards her mother had been setting those relationships up to fail.

Samantha began to think she'd cut off her affections to spite her future.

She knocked again. She loved the people in this house. And they loved her. In their own way. Gabe by default, but wholeheartedly. And Alex cared for her as much as he'd allow himself to care for anyone. With patience and nurturing she could build on that.

Gabe had won him over, was she cutting herself short by not trying harder? After all Gabe had only had his babyish charm, she had intense physical chemistry working for her.

While she pondered the possibilities, a shrill sound, like a cry, came from inside. She opened the door and let herself in. Music and the savory smell of baking meat—Garth Brooks and roasting chicken, two of her favorites—drifted on the air. Odd, considering Alex was going out.

She followed the noise of a struggle to the living room.

What she found melted her heart.

Dressed in jeans and a polo shirt, Alex wrestled on the floor with Gabe and a puppy, the dog little more than a handful of white fur. By the look of it, Alex was losing. The excited cries and yips, the laughter, told her they were having a good time.

How different he appeared from the isolated, controlled man she'd known only months ago. Warmer, more approachable, he laughed easily as he fended off boy and puppy.

Propelled by love, she moved into the room, falling to her knees by the playful threesome. "Alex?" she said loud enough to be heard.

Alex lifted his head and saw her. "Samantha!" He made a grab for kid and dog, and missed. Rolling to a sitting position, he made another grab and snagged the dog. "You're early."

"Mama!" Seeing her, Gabe launched himself into her arms. He pointed to Alex and the wiggling puppy. "Doggy."

"So I see." She relaxed into a cross-legged position. "I was anxious to see Gabe. What's going on, Alex?"

Alex reached out and picked up a single red rose from beside a large white box on the coffee table. He held the rose out to her. "For you."

She cast him a suspicious look. Her glance going from him to the red rose to the big white box with its large red bow to the babies they each held.

"You haven't answered my question. What's going on? Who's cooking? Where did the puppy come from? What about your meeting?"

His cell phone rang. With an apologetic shrug, he

unclipped the phone from his belt and answered. "Hi, Gram. Yes, I know. No, we'll be all right. Thanks for your help anyway."

He disconnected the call, then shut off the phone and reclipped it on his belt. "That was Gram. She called to say she saw you arrive early and to ask if I still wanted her to watch Gabe."

"Alex," she said helplessly, needing to know what this all meant. "I don't understand. I thought I was going to watch Gabe."

"There is no meeting. I wanted to surprise you." He reached out, running a gentle finger down her cheek. "I was hoping we could talk."

Both thrilled by his persistence and confused by waffling emotions, Samantha wistfully bit her lip. Watching him, she bent to smell the rose. Lovely. "And the puppy?"

He reached out for the big white box, placed the tiny dog in the box then he set both in her lap. Taking Gabe at the same time. Meeting her gaze over his son's head, he revealed everything he'd ever held back from her. "The puppy's a symbol of my love for you."

"You got me a dog?" she asked, awed by the gesture. She looked from the sweet bundle of fur to the man sitting anxiously before her. "You love me?" The words escaped, a bare whisper.

He smiled, a pure loving smile. "With all my heart."

Mesmerized by the show of emotion, she leaned over the puppy. He met her halfway in a kiss of intense longing. Of everlasting commitment. Samantha smiled before he fully ended the kiss. He loved her.

For herself.

She cuddled the little dog close. "How precious. What is he?"

Alex rubbed the puppy between the ears. "I'm told he's some sort of terrier." He gathered her and the puppy both into his arms.

"Mama." Gabe launched himself from Alex's arms to hers. Circling his arms around her neck. She hugged him close, carefully juggling baby and dog as she leaned against Alex.

Feeling cherished, she snuggled close, feeling his strength surrounding them all. "Are you sure, Alex?" she had to ask, had to be sure.

"I'm sure. I'm sorry it took me so long to see. So long to say. My only excuse is old habits die hard. You and Gabe changed my life. So fast and so much I had trouble keeping up. You make it look easy. You're so loving, so giving, I didn't see the effort it cost you. I do know how hard it was to live without you, and I never want to go through that again."

"And the baby?" she asked softly.

"I decided on our honeymoon I was ready to have a baby with you. I just didn't know it until this week."

Loving him, wanting everything he offered, she believed. "You realize we're going to have two babies and a dog? Life will not be peaceful."

"You are my peace. As long as I have you, I have everything I need." He kissed her with tender longing. "I love you, Samantha. I want to give you what you've always dreamed about. I want to live the rest of my life with you, our children and Fluffball. Will you have me?''

"I can't think of anything better than spending the rest of my life loving you." Knowing she held everything precious in her life, she wrapped an arm around his neck and drew his head down to hers. Against his mouth she whispered, ''You're better than any dream. You're real.''

*   *   *   *   *

If you enjoyed what you just read,
then we've got an offer you can't resist!

Take 2 bestselling
love stories FREE!
Plus get a FREE surprise gift!

SILHOUETTE *Romance*®

COMING NEXT MONTH

#1718 CATTLEMAN'S PRIDE—Diana Palmer
Long, Tall Texans

When taciturn rancher Jordan Powell made it his personal crusade to help his spirited neighbor Libby Collins hold on to her beloved homestead, everyone in Jacobsville waited with bated breath for passion to flare between these sparring partners. Could Libby accomplish what no woman had before and tame this Long, Tall Texan's restless heart?

#1719 MIDAS'S BRIDE—Myrna Mackenzie
The Brides of Red Rose

Single father Griffin O'Dell decided acquiring a palatial retreat for him and his son was much better than acquiring a wife. But the local landscaper, Abby Chesney, was not only making his home a showplace, she was making trouble! The attractive mother-to-be had already captivated Griffin's young son, and now it looked as if Griffin was next on the list!

#1720 HER MILLIONAIRE MARINE—Cathie Linz
Men of Honor

Attorney Kate Bradley had always thought Striker Kozlowski was hotter than a San Antonio summer—even after he joined the marines and his grandfather disowned him. Now the hardened soldier was back in town and temporarily running the family oil business with Kate's help. Striker didn't remember her, but she had sixty days to become someone he'd never forget....

#1721 DR. CHARMING—Judith McWilliams

Dr. Nick Balfour took one look at Gina Tesserk and realized he'd found the answer to his prayers. After all, what man wouldn't want a stunning woman tending his house? Nick hired her to work as his housekeeper until she was back on her feet. He never anticipated a few kisses with the passionate beauty would sweep him off his!

SRCNM0404